**"Lost?" Leo inquired.
"This is the spice market."**

"I know that," Ellie insisted at once, lying through her teeth since she knew no such thing.

He was lounging against a nearby wall, his tawny gaze fixed on her. His smile deepened and his voice took on a silky note.

"Of course they don't just sell spices here. Women come here from the older parts of the city to buy all kinds of herbal remedies. And they sell cures for other sorts of problems, too. Aphrodisiacs, fertility potions..." His voice trailed away, and Ellie realized that he was gently mocking her.

"I thought it was men who generally needed aphrodisiacs," she said coolly. "Although if that's your problem, I think you'd be better advised to visit a properly qualified doctor."

JOANNA MANSELL finds writing hard work but very addictive. When she's not bashing away at her typewriter, she's usually got her nose buried in a book. She also loves gardening and daydreaming, two pastimes that go together remarkably well. The ambition of this Essex-born author is to write books that people will enjoy reading.

Books by Joanna Mansell

HARLEQUIN PRESENTS

HARLEQUIN ROMANCE

Don't miss any of our special offers. Write to us at the following address for information on our newest releases.

Harlequin Reader Service
P.O. Box 1397, Buffalo, NY 14240
Canadian address: P.O. Box 603,
Fort Erie, Ont. L2A 5X3

JOANNA MANSELL

egyptian nights

Harlequin Books

TORONTO • NEW YORK • LONDON
AMSTERDAM • PARIS • SYDNEY • HAMBURG
STOCKHOLM • ATHENS • TOKYO • MILAN

Harlequin Presents first edition September 1991
ISBN 0-373-11394-3

Original hardcover edition published in 1990
by Mills & Boon Limited

EGYPTIAN NIGHTS

CHAPTER ONE

ELLIE pushed a strand of glossy black hair out of her eyes, stifled a yawn, and tried hard to look alert.

'Well, this is it,' she announced to the group of fourteen-year-old girls clustered around her. 'The treasures of Tutankhamun. It'll take about an hour and a half to see all the exhibition, although we can spend even longer here, if we want to. We don't have to be back at the hotel until half-past five.'

A collective groan went up from most of the girls, and Ellie had to sympathise with them. They had been in Cairo for three days now, and most of that time seemed to have been spent in museums. Ellie had to admit that many of the exhibits were fascinating and impressive, but you could have too much of a good thing!

On the other hand, this *was* an educational trip, not a holiday. The girls had come here to study the ancient cultures of Egypt, which meant they would be tramping round a lot more museums during the next few days.

She decided to start with the Jewel Room. The girls would enjoy the glittering display, and perhaps it would revive their flagging interest in Egyptian relics.

Their eyes definitely sparkled as they pored over the pendant necklaces, the ceremonial jewellery, the exquisite goldwork. The precious stones glittered— cornelian, turquoise, amethyst, lapis lazuli, each one catching and reflecting the light—and Ellie would have loved to have tried on one of the priceless pieces. The

5

room was strictly guarded, though, and the stern-faced men didn't look as if they would consider such a request at all favourably!

Ellie gave a faint sigh. Fascinating though this room was, they couldn't stay here all afternoon.

'Time to move on,' she announced.

The girls reluctantly trailed out after her. Luckily, the next room was as impressive as the Jewel Room. As well as more beautiful jewellery and precious amulets, it contained the famous gold mask that had covered the mummy of Tutankhamun. Ellie had seen countless photos of it, but she had to admit that actually coming face to face with it was something else again.

To her relief, the girls seemed equally impressed. As they began to wander through the other rooms, though, their interest began to fade again. The great war chariots and the throne of Tutankhamun briefly revived their interest, but then they began to chatter among themselves instead of looking at the exhibits.

If it had been up to Ellie, she would have cut their tour short and given them a break from the endless round of museums and exhibitions. She wasn't in charge of this trip, though. Miss Mason, the deputy headmistress of Merralwood School, had arranged it, and set out a rigid schedule for every day they were to spend in Egypt. Ellie had already tried suggesting one small alteration to that schedule, but her suggestion had been curtly turned down. Miss Mason had also looked faintly amazed that anyone should even think of trying to alter her arrangements in any way.

Ellie had got the message, and hadn't tried it again. She was very aware that she was an extremely new— and junior—member of the teaching staff at Merralwood. She had been there for just one term, and was only on this trip because the member of staff scheduled to accompany Miss Mason and the group of girls had been taken ill at the very last moment. It had thrown everyone into a flap because the rest of the staff had already made their holiday arrangements, and Miss Mason hadn't been able to find anyone who had been willing to cancel them in order to go on a school trip! No one, that was, except for Ellie, who had no holiday plans but still hadn't been at all enthusiastic about accompanying a group of teenage girls around Egypt. Since she was on six months' probation, though, she hadn't wanted to do anything that would put this job in jeopardy. She needed it too much. In the end, she had decided she was even willing to face the hassles and traumas of a school trip if it improved her chances of being taken on as a permanent member of staff.

So here she was, in the Egyptian Museum in Cairo, trying to keep a lot of schoolgirls interested in an exhibition of ancient relics. Not easy! she thought to herself ruefully.

Then her attention was caught by one of the girls raising her arm.

'Please, miss,' she said slightly apologetically, 'Sharon's beginning to feel faint.'

Ellie gave a silent inward groan. That was all she needed! She didn't flap, though. This was Sharon's third fainting fit since their arrival in Cairo, and they always rather conveniently seemed to happen when the girls began to get really bored.

On the other hand, there was no point in taking chances. Ellie was very conscious that she was responsible for these girls while they were in her charge.

She went over to take a closer look at Sharon, who didn't look particularly pale or glassy-eyed. The girl gave a couple of faint groans, but Ellie was quite sure she was faking it. She knew that Sharon's main interest was drama, and that she was determined to be an actress when she left school. Well, she should have a flourishing career in front of her, Ellie told herself wryly. She was certainly giving a pretty good performance right now!

Sharon's eyelids fluttered, and she swayed gently. Ellie took her firmly by the arm and began to propel her towards the door.

'You'll be fine once you've had some fresh air,' she said crisply. 'I'll take you outside for five minutes, then we'll rejoin the others for the rest of the tour.'

Sharon sagged limply. 'I'm sure I'll be all right if I can just get out of the museum for a while,' she said in a quavery little voice.

Ellie stifled a grin. The girl deserved an Oscar! When she reached the door, though, she stopped and frowned for a moment. She didn't like splitting up the party, and leaving the rest of the girls on their own. On the other hand, it seemed pointless for them all to tramp out of the museum, stand around until Sharon decided she was feeling better, then tramp back inside again. If only there were some older, responsible-looking person she could ask to keep an eye on them for a short while. There were far fewer people than usual in this part of the museum today, though, and none she would entrust with a group of high-spirited teenagers.

'While I take Sharon outside, I don't want any of you to move out of this room,' she instructed at last, in what she hoped was a very authoritarian voice. Certainly, if Miss Mason had given an order like that, not a single girl would have dared to put a foot outside the door. Ellie suspected, however, that she herself didn't inspire that sort of respect—although they certainly liked her a great deal more than Miss Mason. 'And I want you to take notes,' she went on. She ignored the concerted groan that immediately went up, and added, 'I may well ask you to write an essay about this exhibition once we're back at the hotel.'

She hoped that threat would be enough to keep them in check while she was gone. She turned and began to steer Sharon towards the doorway, but found it blocked by a tall male body.

Tawny eyes stared down into her dark ones, and for a few moments Ellie felt unaccountably confused. Then she got her twitchy nerves back under control again.

'Excuse me,' she said rather stiffly.

The man didn't move out of the way, though. 'Need any help?' he offered. 'I could keep an eye on the rest of the girls, if you like, while you take this wilting little flower outside.'

He aimed a lazy smile at Sharon, who instantly made a remarkable recovery. Her eyelids stopped fluttering, she stood up straight so that she showed off her blossoming young figure to its best advantage, and gave him a quite dazzling smile.

'Not such a wilting little flower, after all,' murmured the man.

Ellie glanced around uneasily, wishing there were more people in this part of the museum. She wasn't sure she could cope if some wolf started stalking her group of girls!

'*Are* you feeling better, Sharon?' she asked sharply.

'Oh, yes!' breathed Sharon. She obviously didn't want to be shunted outside, leaving the other girls alone with this gorgeous man.

And he *was* gorgeous, Ellie conceded rather irritably. And there was a predatory glint in those tawny eyes that told her he was enjoying being in this room full of females.

Only every one of those females, except for her, was under-age! Unless he was very short-sighted—and those tawny eyes didn't give the impression of being in the least myopic—he must know that.

'Cradle-snatcher!' she muttered under her breath.

'I beg your pardon?' said the man politely.

Ellie glared at him and didn't reply. Instead she turned back to the group of girls.

'Come along,' she said crisply. 'Since Sharon's obviously feeling better, we'll move on to the next part of the exhibition.'

'But, miss, I thought you wanted us to stay in this room for a while and take notes,' said one of the girls innocently.

Ellie wasn't surprised to see that it was Donna. Although only fourteen, she could easily have passed for seventeen, and was already showing a very healthy interest in the opposite sex.

Ellie realised that this situation could well get out of hand if she let it go much further. She turned back to the man, who seemed to be thoroughly enjoying the minor disturbance he was causing.

A typically arrogant male! Ellie decided with a sniff. Just because he could turn a few female heads, he thought he was really something!

'Would you mind going away and leaving us alone?' she said in a polite but extremely firm voice. 'This is a school party, and we have a great deal of work to get on with.'

He gently raised one eyebrow. 'Work? In Egypt? Where there are so many fascinating things to see—and do?'

'This is an educational trip, not a holiday,' Ellie informed him curtly. 'And if you don't leave us alone, I'm afraid I'll have to inform one of the museum officials. I won't have these girls harassed by some stranger.'

A smile touched the corners of his mouth. 'Harassed?' he repeated, with obvious amusement. 'I simply offered to help, that was all.'

'I don't need your help.' She hadn't meant to put it quite so bluntly, but she was getting very annoyed by now. It had been a long and tiring day, and she could well do without this sort of problem.

To her relief, the man gave a faint shrug of his shoulders.

'I'll go—if that's what you really want.'

Of course it was what she wanted! Ellie thought with some irritation. She was just about to turn back to the group of girls when the man moved closer and murmured in her ear.

'Your girls were perfectly safe, you know. It was *you* I was interested in.'

Oh, great! Ellie told herself in growing exasperation. That was just what she needed right now, some stranger trying to pick her up!

She was sorely tempted to tell this man exactly what she thought of him. It would be difficult to do that without using the sort of language that the group of girls weren't meant to hear, though! And anyway, when she turned round to glare at him, she found he had disappeared.

She stared at the empty doorway for a few moments in surprise. The man must have moved like some great silent cat. Then she let out a sigh of relief. She didn't really care how or where he had gone. She was just thoroughly glad he had decided not to hang around any longer, causing her even more problems than she already had.

She turned back to the girls, who were looking distinctly disappointed that such a very impressive male should have disappeared so quickly.

'We've wasted enough time,' she said briskly, trying to restore what little authority she had over this group. 'Let's finish this tour, and then we'll head back to the hotel for the evening meal.'

She hustled them fairly quickly through the rest of the rooms. It was fairly obvious that their minds weren't on Egyptian relics, though. At fourteen, they were starting to become more interested and fascinated by the opposite sex than just about anything else!

When they had finally tramped through the last of the rooms housing the treasures of Tutankhamun, Ellie herded them down to the ground floor and then out of the main entrance. Her feet ached, the sun was blazingly hot once they were outside, and she decided she would be very pleased when this afternoon was over. In fact, she was looking forward to the day when this entire trip was over. She hadn't wanted to come on it in the first place. Trudging round a string of museums definitely wasn't her idea of fun.

But then she wasn't sure what *did* pass for fun nowadays, not as far as she was concerned. Life certainly wasn't a bundle of laughs—in fact, hadn't been for such a long time that she couldn't quite seem to remember when she had last got up in the morning and really looked forward to the day ahead.

'You shouldn't frown like that,' advised a voice from just behind her. 'It'll give you wrinkles.'

Ellie recognised it instantly. 'Not you again!' A dark scowl spread across her face. 'I thought you'd gone.'

'I decided to wait outside for you,' replied the tawny-eyed man equably. 'I've already done the rounds of the museum—I didn't want to see any of the exhibitions again. And I hoped you might have dumped that group of schoolgirls by the time you came out.'

'I haven't dumped them and I'm not *going* to dump them,' Ellie retorted. 'I told you, this is a school trip.'

'Surely you get some free time? You can't spend every minute of the day mothering a group of adolescents?'

'Even if I did get some free time, I wouldn't want to spend it with you,' she replied rudely.

'I haven't asked you to—yet,' he replied in a relaxed voice.

She felt herself flushing, which thoroughly infuriated her. And, to make things even worse, the girls were staring with wide, interested eyes at the two of them. She could all too easily guess the kind of remarks she was going to hear whispered behind her back later on!

She moved back a short distance, so that she was at least out of earshot. They might still be able to see what was going on, but at least the little wretches wouldn't be able to eavesdrop as well.

'Look,' she said in a curt, rapid tone, 'I've had enough of this. You're putting me in an awkward situation, and I definitely don't like it. Dragging a group of teenage girls around Cairo is bad enough. Having to deal on top of that with someone who's only interested in a casual pick-up is—is——'

To her horror, she found her voice catching. Oh, this is ridiculous, she told herself miserably. You can cope with this, Ellie. You *can*. You're not going to go to pieces just because some persistent male keeps following you around!

She took a very deep breath and got control of herself again. Then she stared hostilely at the man standing in front of her.

His startling eyes were slightly narrowed now, and fixed on her with a thoughtfulness which she found more than a little disturbing. She wasn't going to let it get to her, though. A couple of months ago she had decided that if she was going to survive in a world that all too often seemed cold and hard, she was going to have to be a lot tougher, a lot less sensitive. Well, now was the time to put some of that resolution into practice!

'I want you to go away and not come back again,' she said in a very clear voice. 'Whatever you're after from me, I'm not interested. And if you *won't* leave me alone, I'm sure the local police would be willing to help get rid of you.'

His tawny gaze glinted briefly. 'Don't act tough,' he said softly. 'It doesn't suit you.'

But Ellie had had more than enough of this by now. 'You can't have the slightest idea what does or doesn't suit me. You don't even know me. And I intend to make sure it stays that way!'

She had half expected an angry reaction. In fact, it would almost have been justified, because she had hardly said a polite word to this man since she had first set eyes on him. Instead, though, he gave an unconcerned shrug, as if her downright rudeness didn't concern him in the least.

'I've obviously picked a bad time for this. I'd better leave you alone for now. I'll see you around.'

Not if I see you first! Ellie muttered under her breath. Then she swung round to find the entire group of girls staring at her with avid interest.

'Let's move off,' she snapped at them, thoroughly rattled by the entire incident.

Donna stared at her in amazement. 'Are you really not going to see him again, miss? But he's the best-looking man we've seen since we arrived in Cairo!'

'When you're a little older, Donna,' said Ellie in her most schoolmistressy tone, 'you'll understand that it's definitely not a good idea to judge men by their looks. Now, let's get back to the hotel straight away.'

The girls chattered and giggled to each other all the way back, and Ellie knew perfectly well what they were talking about. She just hoped that Miss Mason never got to hear about any of this; she lived in dread of doing something that would put her hard-won job in jeopardy.

She found she didn't have much of an appetite that evening, when they all sat down for their main meal of the day. That encounter in the museum had somehow got to her. Damn the man! she thought furiously for the umpteenth time. Why had such an unsubtle attempt at a pick-up managed to get under her skin so much? It was quite ridiculous. After all, she couldn't even remember what he *looked* like by now.

Except for his eyes. She couldn't seem to forget those tawny eyes. In fact, they were the only thing she had really noticed about him. The way they had danced and glinted; the way they had stared at her——

'Not hungry this evening, Miss Mitchell?'

As Miss Mason's cool voice broke into her thoughts, Ellie hurriedly looked up.

'Not very. I expect it's the heat,' she said. And she almost believed her own excuse for her poor appetite.

'I'll be taking the girls to the Museum of Islamic Art in the morning,' Miss Mason went on. 'That means you'll have a couple of free hours. I suggest you spend it reading up on the Pyramids, since that will be our next major trip.'

'Yes, I'll do that,' murmured Ellie, trying very hard to sound enthusiastic and not at all sure she had succeeded.

She didn't sleep too well that night, and deliberately went down late to breakfast the following morning. Miss Mason was an early riser, and insisted that the girls were in the dining-room as soon as it opened to serve breakfast. By the time Ellie arrived, they had already eaten, and had set off on their visit to the museum. For the first time since the school party had arrived in Cairo, Ellie sat down and ate breakfast on her own. What was more, she thoroughly enjoyed it. Food tasted much better when it wasn't eaten under Miss Mason's cold gaze!

She remembered Miss Mason's instructions to read up on the Pyramids, and an unexpectedly rebellious expression suddenly spread over her face. Three days in Cairo, which was meant to be one of the busiest, noisiest, most crowded and fascinating cities in the world, and so far all she had seen was endless museums and the inside of her hotel room!

Ellie decided she could swot up on the Pyramids later. Right now, she was going to make the most of these couple of hours she had to herself.

Where to make for, though? One of the bazaars, she decided at once. She had had enough of culture for a while. She wanted to mix with the local people and soak up something of the atmosphere of this city. And this might be her only chance. She had the feeling that a visit to one of Cairo's markets wasn't marked in on Miss Mason's schedule!

The map in the front of her guidebook told her that it was only a fairly short walk to the Khan el Khalili, which was Cairo's most famous market. She nipped up to her room to change into cool cotton trousers and a loose shirt, slipped a pair of flat, comfortable sandals on to her feet, hurriedly brushed her hair and then left it hanging loose. When she caught sight of her reflection in the mirror, she gave a wry grimace. Miss Mason definitely wouldn't approve of the way she looked right now. Not smart enough—too much like a tourist! When she accompanied the girls on one of their trips, she always had to wear a skirt and blouse, and heeled shoes. Fine in England, but not at all practical in the kind of heat that blazed down on Cairo!

She left the hotel and threaded her way through the streets, quite confident about being out on her own since there were a lot of other tourists about. If she got hopelessly lost, there was bound to be someone who could give her instructions on how to get back to the hotel.

As soon as she reached the bazaar, Ellie knew she was going to love it here. She just wished she had all day to wander through the big covered market, and along the narrow side-streets running adjacent to it, with their tiny shops crammed with gold and silver, perfumes and essences, bolts of brilliantly coloured material, exquisite carpets, glassware, leather goods, and 'authentic' antiques. A lot of the stuff was quite clearly aimed at the tourists who crammed the market, but in between were small gems of genuine craftsmanship.

Ellie lingered over the jewellery and stared rather enviously at the more expensive pieces. One of those gold neckbands studded with bright-coloured jewels would look great against the long glossy strands of her black hair. Not exactly classy, but definitely striking! She could only afford the cheaper pieces, though, and she didn't really want any of those.

Better not start developing expensive tastes, she warned herself wryly. Not on a teacher's salary.

'I'd offer to buy one of those for you, but somehow I don't think you'd accept,' murmured a familiar voice in her ear.

Ellie couldn't quite believe it. The man from the museum? He was *here*? What a lousy coincidence! She had come to the bazaar on the one morning that *he* had chosen to come here.

'I certainly wouldn't accept,' she retorted in a stiff voice. Then she regretted that she had even answered him. She turned her back on him and walked off as quickly as she could, pushing her way through the crowds, but he easily kept pace with her.

'Go away!' she snapped at him. At the same time, she shot a furious glare at him. Why on earth had he had to turn up and ruin her one free morning?

'I don't really feel like going anywhere—unless it's with you,' he told her lazily.

Ellie was beginning to feel distinctly trapped, and she didn't like it. Then she forced herself to calm down a little. After all, what could he do in the middle of these crowded streets? He could make a thorough nuisance of himself, of course, but she wasn't in any immediate danger from this persistent stranger.

Ignore him, she instructed herself firmly. That's the best way to deal with him. No man likes being ignored! It dents their ego too much. Give him the cold treatment, and he'll soon clear off and look for someone else to annoy.

She walked briskly on through the narrow streets and alleys of the sprawling bazaar, stopping every now and then to look more closely at the tempting goods spread out on display. She told herself she was enjoying every moment of her free morning, and that the sights and sounds of the Khan el Khalili were fascinating—even if some of the smells were definitely rather overpowering! Eventually, though, she had to admit she was lying to herself. She wasn't enjoying it one little bit, not since this pest of a man had started tagging along after her.

He hadn't said a word all the time he had been following her, and that unnerved her even more. What did he want from her? Well, whatever it was, he wasn't going to get it, she decided grimly.

In the end, she gave a resigned shrug. Since the morning was ruined, she might as well head back to the hotel. It would take her a while to walk there, and she still had those wretched Pyramids to swot up on before Miss Mason got back.

It was then that she realised she didn't have the slightest idea where she was. She had just walked aimlessly, trying to get away from him, without consulting her map or even really noticing where she was going.

The man gave an infuriating grin.

'Lost?' he enquired, lounging against a nearby wall and fixing his tawny gaze on her yet again.

'Definitely not,' she said coldly.

'This is the spice market,' he told her, ignoring her reply. 'We've come some distance from the main part of the bazaar.'

'I know that,' Ellie insisted at once, lying through her teeth since she knew no such thing.

His smile deepened, and his voice took on a silky note. 'Of course, they don't just sell spices here. Women come here from the older quarters of the city to buy all kinds of herbal remedies. No matter what's wrong with you, someone will offer to sell you an instant cure. And they sell cures for other sorts of problems too. Aphrodisiacs, fertility potions...' His voice trailed away, and Ellie realised that he was gently mocking her, suggesting that *she* might be here for such a remedy.

'I thought it was men who generally needed aphrodisiacs,' she said coolly. 'Although, if you're having those sorts of problems, I think you'd best be advised to visit a properly qualified doctor.'

Not for the first time, she expected an angry re-action and didn't get it. Instead, another of those re-laxed smiles spread across his face, and gold lights glinted in his eyes, making them even more striking.

'How about dropping this war of words and starting over again?' he suggested. 'I'll be perfectly honest. I want a favour from you. And in return, I'll show you the way back to your hotel.'

'You're about the last person I'd ever give a favour to,' Ellie retorted. 'And I don't need any help getting back to my hotel. I've a perfectly adequate street map.'

'Maps aren't much good in a place like this. And the favour's only a very small one. I want to take your photograph.'

'What on earth for?' She was so surprised by his request that she actually forgot to be rude.

'Because it's the reason I'm here. I'm travelling all over Egypt, taking a collection of photographs that will eventually be used in a holiday brochure.'

For the first time, Ellie realised that the camera slung round his neck looked expensive and complicated.

'You're a professional photographer?' she asked.

He hesitated for just an instant, then nodded. 'Leo Copeland,' he introduced himself. 'And the reason I've been following you around is that you've got just the face that I've been looking for.'

Ellie wasn't at all sure that she believed any of this. It sounded too much like a really corny chat-up line! He seemed perfectly serious for once, though, so she eventually decided he must be actually telling the truth.

'What's so interesting about my face?' she said at last. 'It's nothing special.'

Leo Copeland's eyebrows shot up. 'Do you really believe that?'

'Of course I do,' she said rather crossly.

'Then you can't have looked at yourself too closely lately. It isn't just the shape of your face, though. It's your colouring, your eyes—they're all exactly right for what I want.'

'And what *do* you want?' Ellie enquired, a distinct note of caution creeping into her voice now.

'To take some shots of you here, in the bazaar,' he said promptly.

Ellie was still looking at him warily. 'And that's all?'

'Yes—at least, for now,' he answered smoothly.

Her thin, dark brows drew together. She wasn't at all sure she trusted this man. His velvet voice said one thing, but a very different message occasionally flashed from his tawny eyes.

Anyway, what he wanted was out of the question. She could just picture Miss Mason's expression if she opened a holiday brochure one day and saw Ellie Mitchell's face staring back at her!

'No, I'm sorry,' she said with great firmness. 'I can't do it.'

'Why not?'

She began to get annoyed all over again. 'I don't have to give you any reasons!'

'No, I suppose not,' Leo Copeland replied comfortably.

His calm acceptance of her refusal suddenly made her very suspicious. And he looked *far* too smug. Like someone who had already got what he wanted——

'Have you already taken some photographs of me?' she accused, her gaze raking over him furiously. 'Did you snap them before I knew you were there?'

'I did take a few,' he admitted. There wasn't the slightest hint of apology in his voice, which made Ellie even madder. 'I won't use them, though, if you're really set against it.'

'How can I be sure of that?' she demanded.

His gaze became slightly cooler. 'I give you my word.'

She snorted derisively. 'As far as I'm concerned, that means absolutely nothing.'

Leo Copeland's expression altered even further. No laughter in his eyes now, and she was surprised how stern his mouth could look when the last traces of any smile vanished from it.

'What do I have to do to convince you?'

'Give me the film,' Ellie replied immediately. 'That's the only way I can ever be absolutely certain you won't use it.'

She was sure he would refuse outright. His eyes certainly blazed dangerously for a few seconds, and she guessed that no professional photographer willingly relinquished even a few frames of film. Then the flare of light died away again, and he unslung his camera from his shoulder.

'All right,' he said.

Ellie's eyebrows shot up in surprise. 'You'll do it?'

'I've just said I will.' He swiftly and expertly wound the film on to its spool and removed it from the camera; then he tossed it over to her. 'Here—do whatever you like with it.'

Slowly Ellie slid it into her pocket. 'Thank you,' she said in a low voice.

Leo Copeland's gaze ranged thoughtfully over her. 'My offer to show you the way back to your hotel still stands—and no strings attached,' he added, as he saw the wariness flash over her face again.

She longed to turn down his offer, but she *was* lost, and she wanted to be back at the hotel in good time for lunch. Miss Mason didn't approve of lateness.

'If you'll just take me back to the main road, I can find my own way from there,' she said at last.

He gave a brief shrug. 'Whatever you want.'

He set off at a brisk pace, leaving Ellie to scuttle along behind him. She supposed that, now she had refused to be in his photographs, he just wanted to get rid of her as quickly as possible.

The maze of narrow streets and alleys seemed to cause him no problems. He strode on confidently, and in a remarkably short time they were back on a road that she recognised.

'Do you know the way to your hotel from here?'

'Yes,' she said, with some relief.

'Good.' He didn't turn round and walk off, though. Instead, he looked down at her with a quite unreadable expression on his face.

Ellie found it unexpectedly hard to look away from him. And, with her gaze locked on to his, she couldn't help but notice a lot of things that hadn't struck her before.

He had a clever, alert face. Perhaps *too* clever, she thought uneasily. She was already very familiar with his eyes, but she hadn't realised that they were fringed with such long, thick lashes. And his hair was almost exactly the same tawny shade as his eyes, although it glinted with bright highlights, as if he spent a lot of time in the sun. That was confirmed by the dark gold tan of his skin, and the air of health that radiated from him.

She wasn't impressed, of course. Definitely not! The world was full of good-looking men. It was just that she didn't usually see them at such close quarters!

She cleared her throat nervously, and finally managed to force her gaze away from his.

'Er—I'm going now,' she said in a voice that didn't come out quite as firmly as she had intended.

'Mmm,' he said thoughtfully. 'But before you do——'

She wasn't in the least prepared for the swift kiss that followed. She hadn't even seen him bend his head, a predatory light suddenly gleaming in his eyes.

His mouth was warm and hard, and took full advantage of the few seconds it was in contact with hers. Ellie was so startled that she didn't even pull away. Instead, she stood rooted to the spot with astonished shock. She couldn't quite believe that this was actually happening.

When Leo Copeland finally released her, she was just about to splutter out a highly indignant protest when she saw something that made her instead groan in pure dismay.

On the other side of the street, watching her with a whole variety of different reactions, were Miss Mason and the group of girls she had taken to the Museum of Islamic Art.

Leo Copeland raised one eyebrow when he heard her groan. 'It wasn't *that* bad, was it?' he enquired drily.

Ellie didn't even hear him. All she could see was Miss Mason's face, radiating disapproval at full blast.

'Oh, no,' she muttered, briefly closing her eyes. Then she realised that Leo Copeland was still standing extremely close. What if he repeated that kiss? One would be difficult enough to explain. Two would be quite impossible!

'Go away!' she muttered in sudden panic. 'Just *go away*!'

Leo Copeland stared down at her for a few seconds. Then, to her intense relief, he turned round and slowly walked off.

Ellie heaved a huge sigh of relief. That was one problem disposed of. Now all she had to do was try and explain away the incident to Miss Mason!

CHAPTER TWO

ELLIE didn't go straight back to the hotel. She decided to give Miss Mason a chance to cool down before she attempted any kind of explanation.

Instead, she wandered up and down the road outside the hotel, getting hotter and hotter as the midday sun blazed from the cloudless sky. The heat began to give her a steadily increasing headache, and she knew that if she stayed out here much longer she was going to miss lunch.

'This is really stupid!' she muttered to herself. 'I can't parade up and down here all day.'

She took a deep breath and dashed into the hotel. A couple of minutes later, she had made it safely to her room without bumping into either Miss Mason or any of the girls, and she let out her pent-up breath.

This was all Leo Copeland's fault, she thought balefully. Up until now, the school trip had been fairly dull, but at least it had been uneventful. Now she was lurking in her room like some kind of fugitive!

A cool shower and a change of clothing made her feel slightly better. She brushed her black hair until it gleamed, clipped it back since she knew Miss Mason disapproved of it hanging loose, then straightened her crisp white blouse.

She glanced at her reflection and was pleased to see that she didn't look at all like the girl who had been wandering around the bazaar in casual cotton trousers and top, with her hair drifting around her shoulders. Perhaps Miss Mason hadn't even recognised her, she thought hopefully for a moment. Then she wrinkled her forehead gloomily. That was just too much to hope for. And anyway, the group of girls certainly had! Ellie guessed it had been their main topic of conversation ever since.

'Oh, well, you can't go on avoiding Miss Mason forever,' she muttered to herself. 'Time to face the music!'

She forced her legs to carry her down to the dining-room. When she reached the door, she stopped and gritted her teeth for a moment. Then she went in.

Miss Mason and the group of girls were sitting at the long table that had been specially laid out for them. Ellie slid into her seat at the far end, and kept her eyes lowered.

'Sorry I'm late,' she muttered. Then she concentrated on the plate of food that the waiter slid in front of her.

Although she was hungry, she found it surprisingly hard to eat. In the end, she realised it was because she was too tensed-up. Better get this over with right now, she decided with a sigh.

She raised her head and looked straight at Miss Mason. The older woman's face was predictably cold and censorious. Ellie's spirits sank still further, although she hadn't really expected anything else. Miss Mason wasn't known for being kindly and understanding!

'I suppose I ought to apologise for what happened this morning——' she began, a trifle falteringly.

'Not in front of the girls, please, Miss Mitchell,' Miss Mason interrupted curtly. 'We'll discuss this later.'

The girls all looked thoroughly disappointed. They had clearly been looking forward to this confrontation.

Ellie kept her eyes fixed to her plate and somehow managed to finish her meal, although she didn't taste a single mouthful of it. As she swallowed the last forkful, Miss Mason lifted her head and addressed her again.

'You were due to take the girls to the Mosque of Ibn Tulun this afternoon, Miss Mitchell. I've decided that I'll come with you.'

For just a moment, a rebellious light flared in Ellie's dark eyes. Didn't Miss Mason trust her with the girls? What did she think she was going to do? Run off with the first good-looking man who walked up to her? Start kissing some stranger right in the middle of the mosque?

Then her shoulders slumped rather wearily again. She supposed Miss Mason could hardly be blamed for not trusting her. She *had* stood in a public street kissing a stranger. Or rather, she had been kissed *by* him. There was a definite difference—although someone like Miss Mason might not appreciate that!

As soon as lunch was over, they set off for the mosque. The visit turned out to be far more interesting than Ellie had expected, and she would have enjoyed it under any other circumstances. As it was, though, she was very aware of Miss Mason's vigilant eye fixed on her for most of the afternoon. The only time she was free of it was when she volunteered to climb the minaret with a small group of girls who wanted to see the marvellous view from the top. Cairo was spread out all around them, and, although the heat haze didn't allow them to see the Pyramids in the distance, Ellie was still fascinated by the view. It was only spoilt-for her when one of the girls sidled over to her and gave her a frankly curious glance.

'Please, miss—are you going to see him again?' she asked, her inquisitiveness obviously getting the better of her.

'None of this has anything to do with you,' Ellie replied in what she hoped was a very firm voice. 'Please don't ask any more questions about it.'

Disappointment showed clearly on the girl's face. To Ellie's relief, though, she didn't try to push it any further, but went back to join the others.

The rest of the afternoon dragged by, as far as Ellie was concerned. She began to feel as if Miss Mason and the girls were watching her all the time, just waiting for her to put a foot wrong.

You're getting paranoiac! she told herself wryly. And that's ridiculous, because none of it was really your fault. You couldn't have *stopped* Leo Copeland kissing you. It just—well, it just happened! It was simply lousy luck that Miss Mason was standing on the other side of the street, and saw the whole thing.

Ellie squared her shoulders. The solution was simple. Somehow she had to make Miss Mason understand that she hadn't been able to do anything about it. The woman couldn't be *completely* heartless. There must be some way to convince her that Ellie was an innocent party in all of this.

She was highly relieved when it was finally time to head back to the hotel. For one thing, she was terrified in case Leo Copeland took it into his head to come after her again. If he suddenly popped out from behind a corner, Miss Mason definitely wouldn't be amused! She had done all she could to put him off and any other male would have got the message by now. Leo Copeland seemed infuriatingly persistent, though. Not the type to give up easily, once he had decided he wanted something.

When they reached the hotel, Ellie headed straight up to her room to freshen up before the evening meal. She heaved a sigh of relief once she reached it. Not a sign of Leo Copeland all afternoon—perhaps he had finally taken himself off and she could forget about him.

Her cotton trousers and shirt were on the bed, where she had tossed them after changing into the more suitable blouse and skirt that she was now wearing. She picked them up, ready to fold them and put them away. Then she blinked as something small and hard fell out of the pocket in the trousers and rolled across the floor.

Ellie picked it up; then she stared at it with a fresh rush of exasperation. It was the roll of film that Leo Copeland had given her earlier. Just when she had made up her mind to forget him, he had found a way of reminding her of his existence!

She turned the roll of film over in her fingers. Her first impulse was to chuck it into the bin. For some reason, though, she didn't do that. Instead, she stared at the film for some time. Then she pushed it into her pocket.

A glance at her watch told her it was nearly time for the evening meal. Since she didn't want to earn more disapproving glares from Miss Mason by arriving late, she hurried downstairs. As she passed the reception desk, though, she paused for a moment. Then, on an impulse that she didn't really under-stand, she went over to the clerk.

'Can I help you?' he asked with a polite smile.

'I've a roll of film,' Ellie told him. 'I suppose you couldn't—I mean, is there any way I can get it developed?'

'Of course,' said the clerk at once. 'Just leave it with me. It will be ready for you first thing in the morning.'

'So soon?' she said in surprise. She had half expected—half hoped—that the clerk would say it would take several days. Or even that it wasn't possible at all.

He was already taking it from her hand, though, not giving her the chance to blurt out that she had changed her mind, and that she definitely *wasn't* interested in seeing what was on that film.

'First thing in the morning,' the clerk repeated with another smile, obviously pleased that he could be so helpful.

'Thank you,' mumbled Ellie. Then she hurried off to the dining-room, although Leo Copeland had indirectly managed to spoil her appetite for the second day running.

She had her much-dreaded interview with Miss Mason just after the evening meal. She tried to explain exactly what had happened, but Miss Mason wasn't interested in hearing any excuses. She simply set out to impress on Ellie the fact that another incident like that would most definitely not be overlooked. And she succeeded! By the time the interview was over, Ellie was very clear in her mind about a couple of things. Miss Mason expected the very highest standard of behaviour from her staff—and she intended to get it. Otherwise, the member of staff in question would find herself no longer employed by Merralwood School.

Despite all the hassles of the day, Ellie slept soundly that night. As soon as she opened her eyes the next morning, though, she gave a small groan.

'Pyramids day,' she reminded herself as she reluctantly hauled herself out of bed. There were a lot of long, hot and tiring hours stretching out ahead of her.

In between showering and dressing, she thumbed a little frantically through the guidebook, trying to absorb everything it had to say about the Pyramids. Then she shoved the book into her bag, hoping she would have time to take a quick peep at it if any of the girls asked a question to which she didn't have a ready answer.

As soon as breakfast was over, they all assembled in the hotel lobby. Miss Mason was just about to lead the party out of the front door when the clerk came hurrying over to Ellie.

'I have your pictures for you,' he said with a beaming smile.

Ellie briefly closed her eyes. Oh, why did he have to be so helpful?

'Thank you,' she said, grabbing the photos from him and hurriedly stuffing them in her pocket. 'Can I pay you later?'

'Of course,' he said at once. 'Now, if you will excuse me, I have to get back to work.'

As soon as he had scurried off again, Miss Mason's gaze fixed suspiciously on Ellie.

'I didn't know you had a camera, Miss Mitchell.'

'I—I haven't,' Ellie lied a little frantically. 'These are—are just postcards. I haven't had time to buy any during the last few days, so the clerk promised to get some for me.'

She had the horrible feeling that Miss Mason only had to look closely at her face to know at once that she was lying. And what if she demanded to *see* the postcards?

Ellie's nerves twitched frantically, but she needn't have worried. Miss Mason was really only interested in their visit to the Pyramids this morning, and she was already briskly setting off in the direction of the bus station, with the girls trailing behind.

Ellie trudged along after them, a dark scowl crossing her face. She hadn't liked telling that lie. She was normally a very truthful girl, and hated people who lied. It was just one more thing she had to blame on Leo Copeland!

All the same, once they were on the bus she made her way to a seat at the back, well away from Miss Mason. Then she surreptitiously slid the folder of photos out of her pocket.

There were over a dozen of them, and she found she was featured in every single one. She realised now that Leo Copeland must have been following her ever since she had left the hotel that morning, because the first few pictures had obviously been taken in the street leading to the bazaar. Ellie gave a dark frown. She didn't like the thought of any man following her around—and especially not Leo Copeland!

As she flicked through the photos, though, her expression slowly altered. She knew that the girl pictured in them was herself, and yet she just didn't look the way she usually did. Nor could she figure out why. She was more casually dressed, of course, and her hair was swinging soft and loose, but that shouldn't have made that much difference.

And yet she felt as if she were looking at a stranger. Leo Copeland seemed to see her through different eyes from everyone else. He had caught expressions that she didn't know she used, had made her dark gaze look dreamy and far-away, given her a look that was somehow—well, exotic, she thought with a mixture of confusion and embarrassment.

She rather quickly put the photos back into her pocket. For some reason, she didn't want to look at them any more. Instead she stared out of the bus window, catching a glimpse of the Pyramids in the distance, looming yellow against the bright blue sky and then disappearing behind a wall of palm trees as the bus trundled on.

At least today's visit would make a change from all those museums, she told herself with a grimace. And if she could just manage to get Leo Copeland out of her head for the rest of the morning, she might even end up enjoying it.

The bus finally jolted to a halt and Ellie scrambled off. Miss Mason and the girls were already gathered together in a small group, and she hurried over to join them.

The guidebook had warned that they would have to fight their way through an absolute horde of donkey- and camel-drivers, souvenir-sellers, and self-appointed guides—and it hadn't been exaggerating! Yet even the most persistent seemed to crumble and fade away when faced with Miss Mason's stony stare.

All except one, that was. He waited until the rest had slunk away, then stepped forward with a very polite smile. He was wearing traditional Egyptian dress, his robe spotlessly clean, as was his head-covering.

'To see the Pyramids to their best advantage, you need an experienced guide,' he told them. 'For a very reasonable sum of money, I will show you around. I can tell you everything you need to know, and my English is very good.'

His English certainly *was* good, although his accent was quite atrocious. And to Ellie's surprise, she could see that Miss Mason was actually considering accepting his offer.

The tall Egyptian turned to Ellie. Then, to her utter astonishment, he winked at her. She had just begun to glare at him indignantly when she suddenly realised that the man had strange eyes. *Tawny* eyes.

She couldn't believe it! Her gaze fixed intently on his face, searching for something—anything—that would tell her she was wrong.

She didn't find it, though. Instead, she realised she was staring at a face that was horribly familiar. His skin was darker than before—he must have used some sort of dye on it—and his sun-streaked hair was hidden under the loosely wound turban, but she was definitely looking at Leo Copeland!

Ellie wondered for a few moments if she was dreaming. She certainly wished she *were* dreaming; then one sharp pinch would have put an end to all of this. It was all too nerve-rackingly real, though. And, as if to confirm it, Leo shot a lazy and rather smug smile at her, obviously pleased with the way things were going.

Get rid of him, warned a small voice inside Ellie's head. It doesn't matter how you do it—just *get rid of him*.

She turned to Miss Mason. 'I really don't think we need a guide,' she gabbled. 'We can easily find our own way around, and we can get all the information we need from the guidebooks or the Tourist Information Office.'

For a moment Miss Mason looked undecided and Ellie's hopes soared. Then her expression became firm again.

'I think it would be better if we engaged this man to show us around. This is a large site, and he'll take us straight to the parts that are worth seeing. I certainly don't want to waste time. When I worked out my schedule, I only allowed a morning for this visit.'

'And heaven forbid that anything should disrupt that wretched schedule,' muttered Ellie under her breath in exasperation.

Miss Mason's eagle eye fixed on her. 'Did you say something, Miss Mitchell?'

'I just don't think we need a guide,' Ellie repeated stubbornly.

'Well, I do,' Miss Mason said in a tone of voice which definitely discouraged any further argument on the subject.

Leo had been following the exchange with great interest, and he now looked extremely pleased with the outcome. As well he might! Ellie thought balefully. For now, at least, he had got his own way.

But why was he here? What did he want? Those were the questions that were troubling her most of all. What on earth was this charade all about?

She didn't get a chance to ask him because he was already shepherding his little party along the road that led to the Pyramids. Miss Mason strode along beside him, and the girls trotted along behind. To Ellie's relief, none of them seemed to have recognised Leo. That gave her a brief breathing space. All she had to do now was find some way of persuading him to go away before someone else realised that those tawny eyes were very familiar.

She moved a little closer to Leo and Miss Mason, so she could hear what Leo was saying to her. Ellie didn't trust him a single inch. There had to be some reason for this stupid game he was playing, and her nerves were going to keep twitching until she found out what it was.

'It's rather tiring going round the site on foot,' Leo was now telling Miss Mason, still keeping up that appalling English accent. 'Especially in this heat. Would you prefer to ride? I can easily arrange to hire some camels for your party.'

'No camels,' said Miss Mason in a very firm voice.

'Are you sure?' he persisted. 'They are a very practical way of getting around, and really quite easy to ride. Of course, they do sometimes smell a little,' he added apologetically. 'And just occasionally, they spit—although only if they don't like you or they're in a bad mood. But I really think you would get on very well with these animals,' he assured her gravely.

'No camels!' repeated Miss Mason, her tone even more forceful.

Ellie had to stifle an awful impulse to laugh. Then she was rapidly sobered by the thought that this was all a game to Leo Copeland. It didn't matter to him how far he went. It certainly mattered to her, though. After all, her job was at stake here!

They had reached the first of the three Pyramids by now, the Great Pyramid. At any other time, Ellie would have been very impressed and perhaps even a little awed by this massive ancient monument looming up in front of her. Playing the part of the guide to perfection, Leo began to reel off facts and figures. He told them that it was thought one hundred thousand men had worked as forced labour for ten years just to excavate the stone for the Pyramid and transport it to the site. Then it took another twenty years to build the Pyramid itself. Finally he launched into a more detailed description of the Pyramid, its exact dimensions, and its history, finishing with a brief account of the Pharaoh who had been entombed there, Cheops.

Ellie found it unexpectedly fascinating. Or perhaps it was just that Leo had a way of making it all sound so much more interesting than the rather dry words of the guidebooks.

Even Miss Mason looked impressed. Or had she, like all the rest of them, been slightly hypnotised by the velvet cadences of Leo's voice?

'Would anyone like to go inside the Pyramid?' invited Leo. 'You have to pay, but I think you'll find it's well worth it.'

'I believe it's very confined in there, in certain parts,' said Miss Mason, her gaze suddenly flickering uneasily. 'Personally, I've no desire to go crawling round inside. If any of you girls wish to try it, then perhaps Miss Mitchell will accompany you.'

Good heavens, thought Ellie in genuine astonishment. A first chink in that armour! Obviously Miss Mason didn't want to go into the Pyramid because she didn't like confined places. In fact, she had turned quite pale now, at just the thought of entering those claustrophobic passages.

'Well, Miss Mitchell?' said Leo in a soft and yet somehow challenging voice. 'Are you brave enough to venture inside?'

'I'll wait out here with anyone who doesn't want to go,' added Miss Mason. 'We'll take a look at the other two Pyramids while we're waiting for the rest of you to rejoin us.'

Ellie realised that she didn't really have much choice except to venture into the Pyramid. If she refused outright, Miss Mason would want to know why. And Ellie could hardly tell her that she didn't want to go clambering around inside the Pyramid with this guide because he was the same man who had kissed her yesterday!

About half a dozen of the girls finally decided that they wanted to see inside the Great Pyramid. Leo bought the tickets, then led them over to the entrance.

'The passage is very narrow, to begin with,' he warned. 'But there's rather more room once you get further inside.'

None of the girls backed out, and he smiled wickedly at Ellie. 'I think Miss Mitchell and I should go in first. The rest of you can follow along behind.'

Ellie didn't think that was a good idea at all, but this wasn't the time to argue about it. More than anything else, she didn't want to draw too much attention to Leo. Some of the girls had very sharp eyes. It only needed one of them to look at him closely, and there was every chance they would recognise him.

She swallowed hard. Just the thought of it made her throat uncomfortably dry. No one made a fool of Miss Mason and got away with it. If she ever guessed the true identity of their 'Egyptian guide', Ellie definitely wasn't going to enjoy the consequences!

The passage inside was as cramped as Leo had promised it would be. They all had to bend over because the ceiling was so low, and after just a few yards a couple of the girls decided they had had enough. That left just four girls, herself and Leo.

The passage sloped downwards for a while and then began to ascend again, although they still couldn't straighten up. The air inside wasn't particularly fresh, and Ellie decided that the best way to see the Pyramids was definitely from the outside!

'All right?' murmured Leo, so softly that only she could hear.

'No, I am *not* all right,' she flung back at him with quiet vehemence, careful to keep her own voice low so that the girls couldn't hear. 'What the hell do you think you're doing here?'

'I'm showing you around the Pyramids,' he said innocently. 'I think I make an excellent guide. And, unlike most of the other guides, I won't rip you off.'

'How did you know we were going to be here?' she muttered at him.

'I asked a few questions at your hotel. The clerk was most helpful. He knew exactly where you'd be today. He even knew the time you'd be arriving and departing.'

One of the girls behind them moved closer. 'Is it much further?' she asked, putting an end to all the other questions Ellie was itching to ask.

'Just a few more yards, and the passage becomes much less cramped,' Leo assured her.

He was right. Although the passage remained very narrow, the ceiling suddenly soared high up above them, and with a sigh of relief they all stood up straight.

'This passage leads up to the King's Chamber, where you can see the empty sarcophagus,' Leo told them. 'Or there's another low-ceilinged passage that takes you to the Queen's Chamber.'

'The King's Chamber,' voted the girls unanimously. They had had enough of crawling around bent nearly double.

'I'd like to see the Queen's Chamber,' said Ellie, looking pointedly at Leo. She definitely wanted to talk to him alone, and this might be her only opportunity. 'Perhaps you could take me there, while the girls go on ahead to the main chamber.' She turned to the girls. 'Go straight there, then wait for me. And no playing around. Margaret, I'll put you in charge,' she added, nominating the most responsible member of the small group.

The girls set off along the steeply sloping passage, chattering amongst themselves, leaving Ellie alone with Leo.

'Do you really want to see the Queen's Chamber?' he asked, half raising one well-shaped eyebrow.

'Are there likely to be many other people there?' Ellie asked curtly.

'I shouldn't think so. Nearly everyone heads for the King's Chamber.'

'Then that's where I want to go,' she said. 'And please hurry. I don't want to leave the girls on their own for too long.'

'This is looking more and more promising,' murmured Leo, obviously liking the idea of being alone with her. 'And I'm sure the girls will be all right by themselves for a while.'

He headed off down the confined passageway, and Ellie bent over and followed him. Normally, a place like this would have made her feel slightly claustrophobic. It would have been hard not to have been aware of the vast weight of the Pyramid pressing on all sides. Right now, though, she kept her gaze fixed on Leo and didn't even think about it.

They eventually reached the Queen's Chamber, which was a nearly square room with a pointed roof of gigantic blocks. To her relief, it was empty. It would have been hard to have said all she wanted to say if there had been other tourists around.

'Right,' she said, without preamble, 'I want to get a few things straight.'

Leo lounged against the stone wall, not looking in the least out of place in his Egyptian dress. The turban had slipped a little rakishly to one side, and for just a moment it distracted her. It gave him a slightly heathenish look which definitely suited him.

Ellie swallowed hard, and forced herself to concentrate on the matters in hand.

'First of all,' she said, in what she hoped was an extremely firm voice, 'I want you to stop playing these ridiculous games. Following us out here today, dressing up like an Egyptian guide, deceiving Miss Mason and the girls—it's really all been very childish!'

'Yes, I suppose it has,' Leo agreed amiably. 'But it's also been a lot of fun,' he added. '*And* it's meant that we've been able to spend the entire morning together without causing you any problems with the flint-faced Miss Mason.' His eyes narrowed a fraction. 'Why are you so scared of her?' he asked in a rather different tone of voice.

'Because she happens to be the deputy headmistress, and she's got a great deal of influence when it comes to hiring and firing people,' snapped Ellie. 'And, strange though it may seem to someone like you, I want to keep my job.'

'I can appreciate that,' said Leo. 'Why does Miss Mason have so much power?'

'Because Merralwood is a private school. Miss Mason and Mrs Benson, the headmistress, virtually own it and run it between them.'

'Couldn't you get a job at a state school? You're fully qualified, aren't you?'

'Not exactly,' Ellie admitted with great reluctance. 'I finished all the courses, but I—I didn't sit my final exams. They were very short of staff at Merralwood, so they were willing to take me on even though I didn't have any proper qualifications.'

'Why didn't you take your exams?'

'That's nothing to do with you!' she retorted. 'And it certainly isn't relevant to this situation. I brought you here to tell you that you're disrupting this entire trip, and I want you to stop!'

'How am I disrupting it?' enquired Leo with some interest.

She glared at him furiously. 'I'd have thought that was fairly obvious! How can I concentrate on my job when I'm on edge all the time, wondering if you're about to jump out from some dark corner?'

'I suppose I could be very straightforward about this,' Leo said thoughtfully. 'How about if I walk right up to Miss Mason and tell her that I'm extremely interested in one of her staff?'

'No!' squeaked Ellie in horror. 'Anyway, you're *not* interested in me. You can't be.'

'Why ever not?' asked Leo reasonably. 'You don't have two heads, or the kind of face that cracks mirrors. Quite the opposite, in fact. And, as I've told you before, you've got exactly the kind of face that I've been looking for ever since I arrived in Egypt. Very photogenic,' he added, letting his tawny gaze slide appreciatively over her features.

'Oh, don't start that again! I don't *want* to be photographed. Why can't you go and find someone else to take pictures of?'

'Because it's got to be you,' replied Leo in a very calm voice. 'I knew that from the moment I first saw you.'

'That's nonsense,' Ellie retorted crisply. 'There must be dozens of girls who would be just as suitable.'

He shook his head. 'Afraid not. You're the one, Ellie. The series of photos I've got in mind won't work with anyone else.'

'Then you'll just have to forget about them. I haven't got any free time to pose for photos, and even if I had I wouldn't do it!'

His tawny gaze regarded her reflectively. 'Because of me?' he asked at last.

'Yes—no—oh, why can't you get it into your head that I just don't want to have anything to do with you or your wretched photos?' she said in pure exasperation.

Leo gave a small shrug. 'That sounds like a fairly final decision.'

'It *is* final,' she confirmed in a positive tone. Then her eyes met his challengingly. 'Now that you know I'm not interested, are you going to stop all these stupid games?'

'There's no chance that you'll change your mind?'

'None,' she said immediately. She hoped that would be an end to the matter, yet she had the feeling that it wouldn't be. Something in Leo Copeland's face told her he didn't easily give up on anything, no matter what sort of opposition he encountered.

'I'm going to rejoin the girls,' she added shortly. 'I've already left them on their own for too long. I just hope they're all right.'

'I'm sure you can trust them to behave themselves. Although I can't promise the same thing about myself,' Leo added, his tone lowering to an unexpected softness.

Ellie instantly backed away from him, all her nerve-ends radiating warning signals as they reacted to the suddenly husky note in his voice.

'Don't touch me,' she warned, suddenly afraid he was going to try and kiss her again. 'Just try it, and

I'll yell so loudly for help that everyone inside this Pyramid will hear me!'

'Good heavens,' said Leo, with another of those innocent smiles that he seemed to conjure up so easily, 'am I that alarming?'

'I don't know quite what you are,' muttered Ellie, staring at him warily. 'And I don't want to find out!'

'You might enjoy it,' he suggested persuasively.

Her dark eyes became cool. 'I don't think I'd enjoy anything with someone who's got such a very high opinion of himself!'

For just an instant, the warmth left his eyes and Ellie found herself looking at a rather different side of Leo Copeland. Then the smile returned to his mouth and he relaxed again.

'You're a strange girl, Ellie Mitchell,' he told her. 'Difficult, touchy—but definitely interesting. Perhaps that's why I noticed you—why you seemed to stand out from everyone else.'

Ellie stared straight back at him, even though her skin, her muscles, even her spine seemed to vibrate oddly as her gaze locked on to his. She wanted to insist that there was nothing very strange or interesting about her; that most people walked past without even seeing her. So why hadn't he?

Before she could say anything, though, she heard the sound of voices drifting into the chamber. Then a group of tourists emerged from the narrow passage that led to the Queen's Chamber.

Their arrival broke the spell that Leo had begun to spin around her. 'I'm getting out of here,' she muttered. 'I've got to get back to the girls.'

She scrambled towards the passage without even waiting to see if Leo was following her. Quite suddenly, she wanted to get out of this Pyramid and back into the fresh air. She felt as if she would only feel really safe again when she was back with the school group, with Miss Mason's cold stare to keep men like Leo Copeland at bay.

CHAPTER THREE

ELLIE, Miss Mason and the group of girls spent the rest of the morning trudging around the site, gazing up at the other two Pyramids, then staring in some awe at the Sphinx. Despite the crowds of tourists and the commercialisation of the site, its ancient grandeur still shone through. If it hadn't been for the presence of Leo Copeland, Ellie would have enjoyed every minute of it.

Leo was still acting the part of a local guide to perfection. He was polite, helpful and informative, and Ellie was amazed to see that Miss Mason actually seemed quite impressed by him. Leo sensed it too, of course, and played up to it quite shamefully. In a very deferential and courteous way, he even began to *flirt* with Miss Mason, and Ellie inwardly cringed. Any moment now he was going to take the whole thing too far. Miss Mason would either take offence, or, worse still, recognise him. And if that happened Ellie didn't even want to think about the scene that would follow!

To her amazement, though, neither Miss Mason nor any of the girls seemed to realise that this was the same man who had kissed her yesterday in the middle of the street. Of course, Miss Mason had only seen him from a distance, but she usually had *very* sharp eyes. Ellie remained convinced that disaster was going to strike at any moment, though; that Miss Mason would take a good look at him and suddenly see through his rakish disguise.

As the party walked away from the Sphinx, Leo fell back a few paces, and Ellie sidled over to him.

'How much longer are you going to keep this up?' she muttered edgily under her breath.

'I've no idea,' he replied with a cheerful smile. 'As long as I keep on enjoying it, I suppose.'

'Well, I'm definitely *not* enjoying it,' she retorted. 'Although I don't suppose you care about that,' she added a trifle bitterly.

To her surprise, his expression changed. 'Yes, I care about it,' he said in an unexpectedly soft tone. 'But how else am I going to see you? Talk to you?'

'We've already talked!'

'But as far as I remember we didn't actually get anywhere,' he reminded her.

'That's because there's nowhere to go—at least, as far as I'm concerned,' Ellie shot back at him.

Leo shrugged. 'I know—you keep telling me that. But I don't think I can accept it.'

'You've got to!' She tried hard to keep the panic out of her voice, but wasn't at all sure she had managed it.

Leo's gaze flicked over her, and a frown darkened his eyes. 'There's no need to sound quite so scared. What happened to make you so frightened of making any changes to your life?'

'Nothing happened,' she denied instantly. 'And I don't think there's anything very odd about not wanting my life turned upside-down! I've got a job that I want to keep, but if you carry on like this there's a very good chance that I'll lose it.'

'It could be the best thing that ever happened to you,' remarked Leo. 'You're not cut out to be a teacher, Ellie. You're too soft. When these girls get to know you a little better, they'll realise that they can run rings round you—and they'll do it! You're never going to be a Miss Mason, who can bring a whole roomful of adolescents to order with just one intimidating glance.'

Ellie already knew that only too well. In fact, it was one of her most private fears, losing what little control she had over her pupils. And just at this moment she hated this man for actually putting it into words.

'I'm not soft!' she said fiercely, trying to convince herself as much as him. 'And I *will* make a success of this job. At least, I will if you don't get me fired!' she finished angrily.

'Better keep your voice down,' Leo murmured. 'You're starting to attract attention.'

Ellie turned her head and found Miss Mason was shooting a suspicious glance in her direction. She forced the angry expression off her face, then breathed a soft sigh of relief as Miss Mason looked away again.

'There is one way that we can settle this once and for all,' Leo told her.

Ellie was about to insist that there was absolutely nothing to settle, but in the end she saved her breath. No matter what she said, she just didn't seem able to get through to this man. She had never met anyone quite so infuriatingly persistent!

'Give me just half an hour alone with you,' he went on. 'If, in that time, I can't persuade you that you'll have more fun touring around Egypt with me than with Miss Mason and a group of schoolgirls, then I promise to give up and leave you alone.'

'You won't come near me again?' Ellie couldn't quite believe he was making this offer. It sounded too easy.

'I won't come near you again,' he confirmed. 'You won't even see me.'

She was still unconvinced, though. 'How do I know you'll keep your word?'

'You don't. You'll just have to trust me.' His gold eyes met hers and held them, and she was the one who eventually looked away first.

Yet she had the feeling that he was telling the truth, that she *could* trust him. That didn't make her feel any more enthusiastic about accepting his offer, though. And she definitely didn't like the idea of spending half an hour alone with Leo Copeland.

A slow smile spread over his face, as if he could guess what was going through her mind.

'It can be in a public place, if I make you that nervous.'

'You certainly *don't* make me nervous,' Ellie retorted, quite untruthfully.

'No?' His voice lightly mocked her, as if he knew perfectly well she was lying. 'Then why not take up my offer? We can get this finished right here and now.'

'It's quite impossible,' she declared. 'If I suddenly disappear for half an hour, Miss Mason's definitely going to miss me.'

'I can get you away from Miss Mason,' Leo said confidently. Then his eyes met hers challengingly. 'Well? Will you give me half an hour of your time?'

'It won't get you anywhere,' she warned.

'I don't mind taking that chance. As for shaking off Miss Mason for a while, that shouldn't be too difficult. Take off that gold chain around your neck and give it to me,' he instructed.

Ellie muttered rebelliously under her breath. In the end, though, she unfastened the thin gold chain and slipped it into Leo's palm. She had the feeling that people nearly always ended up doing exactly what Leo Copeland wanted.

The chain disappeared into a pocket in the folds of his robe, then Leo quickened his pace so that he caught up with Miss Mason.

Ellie hurried after him. She always got very nervous when he was alone with Miss Mason. She was never sure what tale he was going to spin her next!

'Miss Mitchell appears to have mislaid a gold chain,' Leo was now saying to Miss Mason in an apologetic tone. 'She thinks it might have fallen off while she was inside the Pyramid. With your permission, I'll take her back to look for it.'

Miss Mason immediately looked extremely annoyed. 'Really, Miss Mitchell, this is most inconvenient! And unnecessary. If you'd left your jewellery back at the hotel, this wouldn't have happened. Well, I suppose you'd better go and try to find it,' she said curtly. 'But please try not to be too long.'

'I'm sure we won't be more than half an hour,' Leo assured her smoothly.

Ellie could have hit him. He looked and sounded so sure of himself, and he was obviously enjoying all these games he was playing. As far as she was concerned, though, she was just getting embroiled in more trouble, more lies.

So why was she going along with it?

Because if you can just get through the next half-hour, then you'll be rid of him, she told herself through gritted teeth. He said he'd leave you alone after that. He promised——

Leo turned away and set off in the direction of the Great Pyramid, and Ellie trudged along reluctantly in his wake. She had the feeling that this was going to be one of the longest half-hours of her life!

As they neared the Pyramid, Leo stopped. 'You don't actually want to go inside, do you?'

Since there were far more people outside, and Ellie definitely wanted to stay where there were crowds, she instantly shook her head.

'Of course, we could always climb it,' he suggested.

'It isn't allowed,' she replied promptly. 'It says so in the guidebook.'

'And do you only ever do things that are allowed?' he asked with some amusement.

He was managing to make her sound staid and stuffy, and Ellie illogically resented that, even though it might have been uncomfortably near to the truth.

'I suppose *you've* climbed it,' she said disapprovingly.

'Yes,' he admitted. 'It's pretty strenuous, but the views from the top are stunning.'

'I wish you'd been arrested!'

Leo merely grinned. 'Lots of people do it, and the guards mostly turn a blind eye. But let's forget about the Pyramids for a while. I want to talk about us.'

'There isn't any "us" to talk about,' Ellie responded instantly.

'Why not listen to what I've got to say before you decide that?'

'I don't need to listen to it. I already *know* that I'm not interested in talking to you, being photographed by you——'

'In kissing me?' suggested Leo, his tone lighter than the expression on his face.

Ellie immediately stiffened her shoulders. 'If the rest of the conversation is going to be like this, then we might as well put an end to it right now.'

He looked at her thoughtfully. 'You're very uptight,' he observed at last. 'You'd find life a lot more fun it you loosened up a bit, took things less seriously.'

Quite suddenly, Ellie wanted to yell at him that she *couldn't* loosen up, she just didn't know how. And as for having fun—most days, it was hard enough just to hold things together. Sometimes she seemed to spend every waking minute trying to convince herself that it was all right, she could cope, things *weren't* going to fall apart all over again. And now this arrogant, insensitive man was trying to tell her that she wasn't a fun person. Well, thanks, but she already knew that!

'This is a complete waste of time,' she said in a very clear voice, fighting hard to hold on to her self-control. 'And it's getting us absolutely nowhere. I've already told you that I'm not interested in any of your offers. Why won't you just believe me, and go away?'

'I don't know,' said Leo with unexpected frankness. 'If I had any sense, that's exactly what I'd do. But there's something about you, Ellie, that won't let me give up. And, just occasionally, there's a huge sadness in your eyes. It makes me want to do something about it. Which is rather ridiculous,' he added, 'since I don't even know what caused it in the first place.'

Not for the first time, his sense of perception thoroughly alarmed her.

'Now you're talking nonsense,' she said uneasily.

His tawny gaze seemed to bore right into her.

'Am I?' he challenged softly.

Ellie could feel her throat drying up. She never let anyone get this close to her. She had tried it once, and it had ended in tears and disaster. She wasn't going through all that again.

Leo's eyes took on a brighter hue, as if he knew he was beginning to get through to her. 'Why don't you take a chance and come with me, Ellie?' he coaxed in a low, persuasive tone. 'I'm travelling all over

Egypt. You'd be able to see the country as it *should* be seen, instead of trailing round with a bunch of schoolgirls. And you'd earn good money at the same time. I'd pay you the going rate for a top photographic model.'

His suggestion was absurd, of course. That was why she couldn't understand why it suddenly sounded so very tempting.

She shook her head, trying to clear it. And at the same time she deliberately kept her expression quite blank. She didn't want him to know that she had considered it for even a split second.

'And what would I do when this modelling job is over?' she demanded. 'A couple of weeks of roaming around Egypt, then I'd be back on the dole. Well, no, thanks! I don't want to end up like that again.'

Leo's gaze sharpened. 'You've been out of work before? Why? A bright girl like you shouldn't have any trouble finding a job.'

Ellie could have kicked herself for inadvertently giving that piece of information away to him. And she certainly didn't intend to tell him that employers weren't keen on taking on someone who had got themselves into the sort of emotional mess that she had ended up in.

'Jobs aren't that easy to come by,' she said stiffly. 'Although someone like you might not appreciate that.'

'You seem to think I don't live in the real world,' commented Leo. 'Why?'

Ellie shrugged. 'You wander around the world taking photos, you don't seem to have any ties, any commitments—most people don't live like that.'

He seemed about to say something, then he hesitated. Finally he gave a brief gesture with his shoulders. 'I'm not really that different from other people,' he said at last. 'Believe it or not, I work hard most of the time. And, although I'm not married, I do have the usual family ties—parents, a couple of sisters, handfuls of aunts and uncles and even a couple of elderly grandparents.' He smiled at her. 'You see, we do have quite a lot in common.'

For a few moments Ellie just stared at him. Was he mocking her? Then she realised that he couldn't possibly know. It had only been a bad choice of words. A *very* bad choice of words.

'Family...' she echoed in a voice that, even to her, sounded funny.

Leo immediately caught her strained undertone. 'Is something wrong?' he said sharply.

'No—no, of course not.' She made an effort to pull herself together. This wasn't something she wanted to talk about to anyone, and especially not to Leo Copeland.

'Well, I've heard your offer,' she went on in a deliberately brisk tone. 'And I'm not going to accept it. If there's nothing else you want to say, I think we should go and rejoin the others.'

'You're going to carry on with your dull job?'

'Yes,' she said without hesitation.

Leo continued looking at her in a way that made her want to fidget uneasily. She forced her hands and feet to keep still, and tried to meet his gaze quite steadily.

'Some people are afraid to break away from a boring routine because it's the only thing that holds their days together,' he suggested softly, at length.

'My days are fine, thank you,' she said stiffly.

'And what about your nights, Ellie? What do you do with your nights?'

His gently probing questions had begun to get right under her skin. She decided she had had enough of this—in fact, more than enough!

'I sleep at night,' she retorted swiftly. 'Not that it's any of your business!'

Leo ignored her last remark. 'And do you sleep well?'

'Extremely well!' Ellie thought she had rarely told so many lies as she had the last couple of days. There was no way she was going to admit the truth to this man, though.

For just an instant she wondered if he had believed her. Then she decided that she didn't really care either way. She had turned down his absurd offer to go trotting all round Egypt with him, so that should be an end to the whole ridiculous affair. And there were only a few minutes left now of the half-hour she had promised him. She was nearly safe.

Safe? The word echoed round inside her head again, making her wonder why she had used it. Had she ever been in any danger?

Of course not, she decided firmly. She was just being over-imaginative. Perhaps this place, with its fantastic monuments and its sense of history, was beginning to get to her. And it was very hot. It was easy to be over-dramatic in those circumstances.

She looked up at Leo, and found that he had moved closer. She didn't like it when he did that. For some reason, it made her remember that kiss he had given her.

Forget the kiss. Forget him! she ordered herself sharply. Get back to Miss Mason and the girls, before this man springs any more surprises on you.

'I think your half-hour's just about up,' she informed him, managing to keep her voice very cool.

Leo glanced at his watch. 'Not quite. I think I've still got a couple of minutes left.' The sun glinted on his eyes, giving them a golden sheen. 'How do you suppose we should spend them?' he enquired in a voice that was suddenly lined with pure velvet.

Ellie swallowed hard. She wished he wouldn't use that tone of voice. She was certain he was doing it deliberately, and it seemed to do extraordinary things to her nerve-ends.

She wondered if he could sense her confusion. She was sure he could, and that began to make her angry—although she didn't know if it was with him, for provoking that reaction, or with herself for letting him see it.

She turned away from him and began to walk off. If she didn't say one more word to him, perhaps he would get the message and finally *leave her alone*.

A few seconds later, though, a shadow swept over her. And she knew at once who that shadow belonged to. She stubbornly refused to turn her head and look at him. In fact, even if she had, she wouldn't have seen him very clearly. Her eyes were starting to blur, as the whole stupid, farcical situation began to grate badly on her nerves. All of a sudden she felt horribly vulnerable, and a wave of familiar misery slowly began to roll over her.

Oh, no! she thought in growing panic. Not here. Not now! She had thought she was over those fits of depression which, at the lowest point of her life, had just arrived out of the blue and bowled her over. She had forgotten that they had most often hit her when she was on edge, tired or uncertain. And, because she had been free of them for several months, she had stopped being on her guard against them.

'What is it?' asked Leo in a rather abrupt voice.

Although she wasn't looking at him, she knew he was staring at her with some intensity.

'Nothing,' she managed to get out. 'It's probably— just the heat.' That seemed like a perfectly good excuse to her, so she clung on to it. 'Yes, it's the heat,' she insisted in a voice that still wobbled. 'It's making me feel a bit—a bit woozy.'

Leo hooked one hand firmly under her arm. 'Then the first thing is to get out of the sun,' he told her, and he steered her over to a nearby patch of shade.

It was a relief to get out of that hot, bright glare, and Ellie actually felt slightly better as she felt her burning skin begin to cool.

Maybe it really *was* the heat, she told herself. Her eyes were starting to clear again, and her nerves felt a little less raw than they had a few moments ago. She let out a long, slow sigh of relief as she got control of herself again; then she realised that Leo was still holding on to her arm.

'You can let go of me now,' she told him, rather more sharply than she had intended.

'I think I'd better hold on to you a little longer,' he decided. 'Heatstroke can be a funny thing. You think you're OK, but then you just keel over. I want to make sure you're absolutely all right before I let go of you again.'

His grip was far too firm for her to shake herself free of it without an awkward and undignified struggle. And it was odd, but it was just after he had taken hold of her that she had begun to feel better.

It had to be a coincidence, Ellie told herself uneasily. He wasn't some sort of magician. He couldn't get rid of a fit of depression with just the touch of his hand.

Leo fished inside his robe and brought out the gold chain he had taken from her earlier.

'Here, you'd better have this back,' he said. 'We don't want Miss Mason to think that you've been away all this time without good reason!'

Ellie stared at the chain for a few moments. Then she remembered that it had been their excuse for getting away for the half-hour that Leo had demanded to spend with her. She was supposed to have lost it, and gone to try and find it.

The chain sparkled in his tanned fingers, a dark gold that matched his eyes.

His fingers slid gently round her neck. 'You'd better let me fasten it for you,' he said softly.

Ellie meant to say she could easily fasten it herself, but somehow the words didn't come out. His fingertips grazed her throat, slid across her warm skin, and seemed to take a very long time to clip the simple clasp together.

An involuntary shiver ran through her, and Leo looked at her in some surprise. He didn't remove his fingers, though, and Ellie didn't draw back from him, although she knew she should.

They stood together for several more seconds, lightly linked by the touch of Leo fingertips against her glowing skin. Then common sense began to filter back into Ellie's whirling head and she hurriedly shook herself free of him and took a step back.

What on earth was she doing? she demanded of herself with a rush of shock. She was meant to be putting as much distance between this man and herself as possible, not letting him get even closer to her!

'There's still time to change your mind, Ellie,' Leo told her in an unexpectedly quiet voice. 'You can change your whole life right this minute—if you want to. Just hand in your resignation, and come with me.'

But the moment had passed. The old Ellie was in control again now, the Ellie who craved some kind of stability and security in her life, even if it was only a job that she didn't really like and which had very few prospects.

'I don't want to change anything,' she said stubbornly. 'And your half-hour's definitely up now. Goodbye, Mr Copeland.'

She walked firmly away from him, ignoring any impulse to look back. And this time, to her relief, he didn't follow her.

A few minutes later she rejoined Miss Mason and the group of girls.

'Did you find your necklace?' enquired Miss Mason.

'Yes—yes, I did,' said Ellie, a little guiltily.

'You've been rather a long time.'

'Sorry,' she apologised. 'I—I didn't feel too well. The heat——'

Miss Mason peered at her. 'You do look rather pale,' she said with a frown. 'I hope you're not coming down with something. It really would be most inconvenient if you were taken ill.'

'I feel much better now,' Ellie said quickly. 'I think I've just been out in this hot sun for too long.'

'Perhaps you'd better stay at the hotel and rest this afternoon, just as a precaution. I'm taking the girls back to the Egyptian Museum for a couple of hours, but I dare say I can manage on my own.'

Ellie was about to say that she felt well enough to cope with the afternoon's trip, but at the last moment she shut up. The prospect of a few hours to herself was too irresistible. After the last fraught couple of days, it was exactly what she needed to get her overstretched nerves back into some kind of order.

They arrived back at their hotel in time for a late lunch. Ellie wasn't hungry, but she forced down some food. And she cheered herself up with the thought of the free afternoon that stretched ahead of her.

She heaved a huge sigh of relief as she saw Miss Mason and the group of girls finally go trooping out of the front door. Miss Mason had given her strict instructions to go and lie down in the cool of her air-conditioned room for the rest of the afternoon. Ellie didn't think Miss Mason was suddenly having a change of character and showing real concern, though. She was simply worried by the thought of Ellie falling ill. She didn't relish the prospect of single-handedly having to shepherd a party of rather unruly school-girls around Egypt.

In the end, Ellie did go up to her room. She just didn't feel in the mood to face the heat and noise of Cairo's crowded streets. Instead of resting, though, she took a long, leisurely shower and washed her hair.

After drying herself, she pulled on a cool cotton robe, then sat in front of the mirror, slowly pulling a brush through the long dark strands of her hair as she let it dry.

Her reflection in the mirror caught her attention, and she looked at it with detached interest, as if it belonged to a stranger. Then, after a couple of minutes, she put down the brush and crossed the room.

She dug out of her bag the photos that Leo had taken of her. Then she went back to the mirror, studied her reflection again, and compared it with the girl in the photos.

She didn't know why, but it didn't quite seem to match. She just wasn't the same person that Leo had caught with his camera.

She found herself wondering which was the real Ellie. Then she shook her head with a touch of exasperation.

You are, of course, she told herself firmly.

Then who was the girl Leo had seen? Ellie didn't know, but she was oddly fascinated by this other side of her that no one except Leo Copeland seemed to see. And the idea of somehow becoming that new Ellie—that different Ellie—held an unexpectedly strong appeal.

She stared at the familiar lines of her face again, then smiled.

I think you're becoming a little crazy, she lectured herself. There's only one of you. A rather dull girl of twenty-three with a rather dull job!

Then her smile disappeared. Crazy—that had been the wrong word to use. It was a word that she tried to avoid whenever she could. There had been times last year when a genuine craziness had come far too close for comfort.

The memory of that abrupt fit of depression this afternoon crept back into her mind, and a disturbed expression entered her dark eyes. *Had* it only been the heat that had caused it? Oh, please, let it just be that, she prayed silently. She really didn't think she could go through all that again.

But if it hadn't been the heat, what else could have triggered it off?

Ellie knew the answer to that question only too well. It had been Leo, talking about his family.

Family—another word she didn't like to use or hear. Because she didn't have any. Not one single person in the world who was related to her, or truly cared about her. And it was the one thing that she still found so hard to come to terms with—the feeling of utter loneliness, utter isolation. Most of the time now, she could cope. If she hadn't learnt to cope, she would have gone under completely. Nearly *had* gone under completely. But there were still certain times of the year—Christmas, birthdays, special occasions—when it got to her all over again, as sharp and painful as it had been right at the beginning.

She had had a family once, of course. A father and mother, a younger sister—all long dead now, victims of a hotel fire. A holiday that had turned into a disaster, and Ellie had only escaped because she had caught chicken-pox and hadn't been able to go with them. Sometimes, irrationally, she still felt guilty. They were dead, and she was alive because of catching a silly childhood disease.

She had gone to stay with her grandparents while her parents and sister were away. After the dreadful news had come through, she had stayed with them. An eight-year-old who hadn't really understood what was happening, who still went on expecting her mother and father to come walking through the door even though people had gently tried to explain to her that they wouldn't be coming back.

And, slowly, she had come to accept their absence, even though it never stopped hurting. She had grown up and adjusted to her new life, and been grateful that at least she had her grandparents to care for her and love her.

But they had both been elderly, and with fearful eyes she had watched them grow more and more frail. Her grandfather had died first, peacefully in his sleep. Then, during her last year at teacher-training college, her grandmother had had a heart attack, and that had been that. The one thing that Ellie had feared more than anything had finally happened. The last of her family had gone, leaving her totally alone in the world.

Except she wasn't *quite* alone, because by then Steven had come into her life. She had met him during her last year at college, and had fallen for him at once. And, as well as being good-looking and charming, Steven had one other enormous asset. He had a big family who always welcomed Ellie with open arms whenever he took her home for a couple of days.

She knew that, if she married Steven, she would have a family again. People who would be there if she needed them.

Perhaps that was why she had pushed their relationship just a little too hard. She knew she was doing it, even knew it was driving him away from her, but she couldn't stop. She needed someone so badly that she just wouldn't accept that Steven wasn't ready yet for marriage.

In the end, of course, the inevitable happened. He got tired of the constant pressure and decided he could do without it—and without her.

And then Ellie truly *was* on her own. And that had been the most awful time of her life. She had friends, of course, but they weren't enough. She needed more, so much more, and fell apart when she realised she couldn't have it.

She recognised now that she should have had professional counselling. It wouldn't have cured the loneliness, but it would have helped her to come to terms with it and shown her how to live with it. Instead, she dropped out of the teacher-training course just a week before her final exams—and then dropped out of life.

It had been the lowest, loneliest point of her life, and it had gone on for nearly six months. She hadn't been able to hold down a job; had lost contact with most of her friends; had only just managed to survive on the unemployment money which she'd hated claiming but had needed, because she'd had no other source of income.

Then slowly, very slowly, she began to pull herself out of the trough of depression she had tumbled into. It had been incredibly difficult, but she had grimly persevered because she had suddenly become very frightened of the alternative. And finally there came a day when she could face the world again; could even begin to live in it. She even felt confident enough to look for a job. *Needed* a job, to complete her recovery. Only it was hard to find one because she had no experience, no qualifications.

An old friend from college, who knew about the rough time she had been through, had told her about the vacancy at Merralwood School. She had somehow summoned up enough nerve to go for the interview, and no one had been more surprised than Ellie when she had got the job. And it had turned out to be a lifeline. Hard at first, of course—*very* hard, and there had been times when she had felt like giving up. But she had struggled on through the bad parts, and finally she had won through. Life was still hard, but now she could cope with it. It wasn't fun, but she didn't expect fun. In fact, she had almost forgotten what it was like. But at least she could get through the days now—and the nights—and as far as she was concerned, that was a major achievement . . .

A knock on the door interrupted her thoughts and brought her sharply back to the present. She glanced up and frowned. Room service? But she hadn't ordered anything.

Then she wondered if Miss Mason had asked them to bring her an afternoon cup of tea. It wasn't like her to be so thoughtful, but she might have acted out of character for once!

Ellie went over and opened the door. Then her features became set as she found herself staring straight at Leo.

He was still wearing the Egyptian robe, although he had abandoned the turban, and his tawny gold hair shone brightly against the dark dye that covered the skin of his face.

'I don't believe this,' Ellie said coldly. 'I thought I wasn't going to see you again.'

'So did I,' Leo replied slowly. 'But there was something about you today that bothered me. I got the feeling that you shouldn't be left on your own.'

It deeply disturbed her that he was capable of these flashes of insight.

'I'm perfectly all right,' she insisted, keeping her eyes lowered so that he wouldn't be able to read them.

'Are you?'

'Yes!' she said with some vehemence. Although she wasn't certain if she was trying to convince him or herself.

Leo studied her for a few more seconds. Then he shouldered his way past her and came right into the room.

'You can't do this!' she snapped furiously. 'You've got no right!'

'No, I haven't,' he agreed. He walked over to the window, then turned to face her. 'But I'm not going to leave until I'm sure you're OK.'

He sat down, looking as immovable as a mountain, and Ellie's heart seemed to sink several feet. What on earth could she do about this man?

She would ignore him, she decided shakily. She wouldn't say a single word to him. Eventually, he would be bound to get fed up, and leave.

She began to brush out her hair, which was still slightly damp, and pretended she wasn't aware of that tawny gaze fixed on her. It was all a question of will-power, she told herself a little desperately. Sooner or later, one of them would get tired of this deadlock.

And she was determined it wasn't going to be her.

CHAPTER FOUR

AFTER a few minutes, Leo turned his head and gave her a quizzical glance. 'Are you going to keep up this silly silence all afternoon?'

Ellie didn't even look at him. She was carefully applying make-up now. Not too much, of course. Miss Mason didn't actually approve of any make-up at all, but would just about tolerate the dusting of gold shadow that highlighted the darkness of Ellie's eyes, and the touch of lipstick that lent a soft sheen to her lips. She didn't need blusher. Her cheekbones had already caught the sun, which had given them a light coating of colour. And even if they hadn't, Ellie had the feeling that Leo's presence would have been enough to have given them a bright glow.

'This is rather a waste of precious time,' Leo went on in the same light conversational tone. 'With Miss Mason safely out of the way, we could be doing something much more interesting than just glaring at each other.' As Ellie continued to ignore him, a slow smile spread across his face. 'Admit it, Ellie. Once you stopped being scared of the old dragon, you had fun this morning. Probably the most fun you've had since you started out on this trip.'

Again, Ellie didn't answer, but this time it was because she didn't want to admit to him that there had been moments when a perverse part of her *had* enjoyed it. And there had even been something oddly enjoyable about the tension, wondering all the time if Miss Mason was going to catch on and positively explode with furious anger and disapproval.

You must be mad! she told herself wonderingly. How on earth could you possibly have enjoyed one minute of a situation which could easily have ended with you losing your job?

She didn't know, and that distinctly unnerved her. Just as this man unnerved her. If only he would get out of here! What if Miss Mason returned early, and came up here for some reason? Ellie could all too vividly imagine the expression on Miss Mason's face if she walked in and saw Leo lounging elegantly in the chair, looking completely at home in Ellie's room!

She glanced up and found his tawny gaze was locked on to her face again now. It was something that seemed to be happening more and more often, and Ellie didn't like it. She could never be absolutely sure what he was seeing. Those golden eyes seemed to probe right underneath the surface and pick up information that other people wouldn't see in a lifetime of knowing her.

Leo got to his feet, and she jumped nervously. He noticed it, of course—the wretched man seemed to notice everything!

'Do I set your nerves that much on edge?' he asked with a faint frown. 'I don't like to do that to any woman. And especially not to you, Ellie.'

He came a little closer and, without realising she was doing it, she began to twist her fingers together edgily.

'Do *all* men make you this nervous?' he questioned softly. Then he answered his own question. 'No, I don't think so. Just me.'

She cleared her throat, not wanting her voice to come out in a betraying croak.

'I think you're flattering yourself,' she said, making a huge effort to stay outwardly very cool.

'Possibly,' he agreed in an untroubled tone. 'But I don't think so. I'm good with women, Ellie. I like them, so I find it easy to tune into their moods. I'm getting some very odd signals from you, though. I can't quite figure them out. I *do* know there's something disturbing you, though.'

'You're right about that,' she retorted. 'It's the prospect of losing my job! Miss Mason's got pretty strong views about members of staff who entertain men in their room!'

'But Miss Mason isn't here right now,' Leo pointed out easily. 'It'll be another couple of hours before she gets back. So, if there's anything around here that's disturbing you right at this moment, I think it's got to be me.'

'You really have got a high opinion of yourself,' Ellie said scathingly. 'You seem so sure that you're all I think about. Well, I've news for you, Mr Copeland—as far as I'm concerned, you're not that important.'

If she had hoped he would react angrily to her words, it was fairly obvious she was going to be disappointed. His eyes glinted brightly for the very briefest of moments. Then his features took on that unflappable expression which irritated her intensely, for some reason. What *did* she have to do to provoke this man, and get him to stride off in a fit of temper, swearing he wouldn't come near her again?

'I think you should call me Leo,' he told her, calmly ignoring her last outburst. 'There's really no point in being so formal.'

'I prefer to call you "Mr Copeland",' Ellie insisted stiffly.

His eyebrows lifted lazily. 'In that case, I'm going to have to teach you how to unbend a little. You see,' he added, moving closer, 'I want to hear you say my name.'

Ellie hastily took a step backwards, because there was a much more purposeful set to his face now, and a velvet undertone to his voice that was beginning to sound very familiar.

The back of her legs hit something, though, preventing her from retreating any further. She glanced round and, with a small gulp, realised she was standing right by the bed.

Not a good place to be! she told herself shakily. It didn't take much to give Leo Copeland the wrong idea. Seeing her standing beside a bed could put all sorts of very unsuitable notions into his head!

She started to sidle away from it. She expected him to move in front of her and block her, but to her intense relief that didn't happen.

Rather hurriedly, she walked over to the window. She felt much safer there. Then she realised that Leo had followed her. He had moved at a very leisurely pace, which was why she hadn't realised straight away that he was closing in on her again. It was almost as if he didn't want to make any sudden movements which would make her even more nervous.

And she *was* nervous, she conceded with a dry swallow. She didn't exactly know why, either, which only added to her overall sense of deep unease.

Leo loomed nearer, and she realised that he was actually a deceptively big man. She was five foot eight inches in her stockinged feet, but he was still a head taller than she was. And his shoulders, although not particularly broad, still somehow gave the impression of being extremely powerful. Not an easy man to get away from, if he decided he didn't want to let her go.

'I wish you'd stop following me around,' she said in a low and rather unsteady voice.

'And *I* wish you'd call me Leo,' he reminded her.

Ellie stared up at him warily. 'If I agree to do that, will you leave me alone?'

A slow smile stretched the corners of his mouth, giving it a positively wolfish set. 'Not necessarily,' he said softly. 'You see, I'm beginning to realise that the kiss I took from you the other day wasn't quite enough. It's just left me with a taste for more.'

Ellie was beginning to feel very vulnerable, and she didn't like it. And the reason she didn't like it was becoming increasingly clear. It was because she wasn't as angry with this man as she should have been. If any other virtual stranger had come in here and told her he wanted to kiss her, she would have told him clearly and concisely that she wasn't interested. That if he didn't get out of here immediately, she would call the hotel manager. Or yell the place down if she still didn't get the message.

Leo Copeland didn't make her want to do either of those things, though. She knew she *should*—but she just didn't want to.

It was all very unsettling. But not quite as unsettling as the hot glow that had begun to light Leo's eyes.

Ellie discovered that her legs had begun to feel peculiarly weak—almost as if she needed something to cling on to. But the only solid object near to her was Leo, and she definitely didn't think it would be a good idea to cling on to him!

She had been expecting him to carry out his threat to kiss her. When it didn't happen straight away, she began to feel a little less shaky. Perhaps he had only been joking. Then she dismissed that comforting thought and forced herself to be on her guard again. Don't ever underestimate him, she warned herself. And, above all, don't let him get to you!

Because she had already realised that this was something Leo Copeland would be very good at. In fact, she had the feeling that women were his speciality.

Men like this were highly dangerous, she decided with a distinct gulp. And *not* the type that she should ever get involved with.

Leo was watching her with quiet amusement, as if he was almost enjoying the struggle that was going on inside her head.

'Right at the moment, you look very confused,' he told her. 'Perhaps it's time I tried to put a few things straight for you.'

Then he *did* kiss her. And, although Ellie had been expecting it, it still threw her completely off balance.

She had been right all along, she thought a little wildly. This man *was* highly dangerous. And definitely not to be trusted.

Then his kiss deepened, which left her with very little opportunity to think about anything else at all.

She soon realised that he was very, *very* good at this. But she had known all along that he would be. Even that brief kiss he had given her before had had all the unmistakable hallmarks of the expert.

His mouth didn't demand or intrude. It simply caressed. He seemed to know that gentleness was the one thing she would find quite irresistible.

'Nice?' he murmured enquiringly, lifting his mouth from hers for the briefest of moments.

Ellie gave an indistinct gurgle, but he seemed perfectly satisfied with that unintelligible response.

'I think so too,' Leo agreed. And, before Ellie had a chance to say she hadn't meant that at all, his lips returned to hers with much more force and purpose.

She still didn't understand how this could be happening. How she could be *letting* it happen. She wasn't a teenager, dazzled by a first kiss.

Only somehow that was just how it felt. As if it had never happened before. As if all the other kisses in her life had just been wiped out.

Leo's hands, which had been resting lightly against her waist, moved softly upwards, pausing just beneath the swell of her breasts.

She shouldn't let a stranger touch her like this, Ellie told herself a trifle dazedly. Only it was becoming increasingly hard to think of Leo as a stranger. Almost impossible to believe that she hadn't even seen him until a couple of days ago.

His fingers grazed fleetingly against the softness of her flesh and she felt an extraordinary impulse to relax and purr with contentment. His touch was incredibly soothing. Steven had never made her feel like this——

As soon as she thought of Steven, though, she instinctively tensed up again. She felt no bitterness towards Steven—*she* was the one who had messed things up between them by wanting too much from him, demanding something that he just hadn't been ready to give. Just thinking about him trawled up all the other bad memories, though, and brought her sharply back to reality.

'Stop touching me like that!' she said sharply. At the same time, she tried to push Leo's hands away.

But he wasn't ready to let go of her yet.

'A moment ago you liked it,' he reminded her, his breathing coming a little faster now.

'A moment ago I was a little crazy!' Ellie retorted. 'But now I've got my head straight again and I can see what you're up to.'

'And what exactly is that?' Amusement coloured his voice again, although his breathing still wasn't entirely steady.

'You're trying to—to——'

'Seduce you?' he finished for her, as she went bright red trying to find the right words. 'No, Ellie. You're not ready for that yet.'

'Too right I'm not!' she retorted. 'And I never will be, where you're concerned.'

'You didn't like being kissed by me?'

'No!' Then she went an even deeper shade of scarlet and wondered, a little desperately, how many more lies she was going to have to tell before she managed to get Leo Copeland out of her life.

One tawny eyebrow slid skywards. 'You really didn't like this?'

His mouth swiftly covered hers again, leaving her with no time—or inclination—to repeat her protests or her lies.

This kiss was bone-shakingly different. A small taste of what Leo was capable of, if he really put his mind to it. His tongue probed and teased with frightening effect, his hands moved with a new and nerve-numbing confidence, and Ellie was devastated to feel her treacherous body relaxing into quite terrifying compliance.

If only he wasn't getting right inside her head and somehow affecting her *there*, she thought with a touch of despair. She could have coped with the physical side of this. Steven had taught her about desire—

although rather clumsily, she sometimes admitted when she allowed herself to think of their time together.

Yet this wasn't anything like the rather mild sensations Steven had aroused in her. This was—so much more vivid, more primitive, like a wildfire that would race out of control the instant it was given a chance.

So don't give it that chance! she instructed herself, somehow dredging up a new surge of resistance. Or you're going to end up in terrible trouble.

With an almost superhuman effort, she forced herself to ignore the trails of heat that Leo's fingers ignited as they moved over her quivering skin. When his mouth began hunting for hers again, she turned her head away and doggedly ignored his grunt of frustration. And finally she managed to extricate herself from the increasingly possessive touch of his hands, and slid away out of reach when he tried to pull her back again.

'I could have you charged with assault!' she threw at him, in a slightly frantic attempt to keep him away as he began to move purposefully towards her again.

That stopped him in his tracks. He stared at her in amazement for a couple of seconds. Then, disconcertingly, he threw back his head and laughed.

'I'm glad you find this so amusing,' she said cuttingly, beginning to get control of herself again now that she was free of the seductive touch of his lips and hands.

'It might be even more amusing if you weren't so very serious about it,' Leo replied, his eyes still bright, but losing the glow that had lit them only seconds ago.

Ellie drew herself up to her full height, which still left her at a distinct disadvantage since it barely brought her up to his shoulder. She knew she had to get out of here while she still had some sort of control over the situation.

'Since I can't physically throw you out of here, I intend to leave myself,' she informed him in a voice that sounded unnervingly like Miss Mason's at its most frosty. 'I'm going down to the hotel lounge. At least you won't be able to pester me there!'

'Run away, if you like,' said Leo in an unexpectedly relaxed tone. 'But I think you should put some clothes on first.'

Ellie glanced down at herself, and her mouth dropped open in pure dismay. She was still wearing the bathrobe that she had put on after her shower. No wonder Leo had enjoyed touching her. There had been nothing between his fingers and her bare skin except a very thin layer of cotton!

She could feel her face positively flaming, and was furious that he could provoke this schoolgirlish reaction from her. Muttering balefully under her breath, she grabbed some clothes and scurried into the bathroom. It took her only seconds to dress. Then, her dark hair flying loose around her shoulders, she went back into the bedroom.

She didn't even look at Leo. Instead, she whipped up her bag and headed straight for the door.

When she was halfway out of the room, though, she stopped and shot a dark backward glance at him.

'I expect you to be out of this room—and out of this hotel—in ten seconds flat,' she hissed at him. 'And you may be "good with women", Mr Copeland, but this particular woman doesn't want to see you ever again!'

She slammed the door shut behind her and almost ran down the stairs. She half expected him to come after her, but she reached the bottom without hearing any sounds of pursuing footsteps, and when she glanced round there was no sign of Leo Copeland.

Slowly getting her breath back—although her pulses were still thumping—she made her way to the hotel lounge. To her relief, there were a couple of people already there, one reading a newspaper and the other dozing in a chair. At last she felt safe. Even if Leo did follow her, he wouldn't be able to lay a finger on her, not while there were other people around.

Ellie collapsed into a chair, picked up a newspaper and made a pretence of reading it. She didn't take in a single word of the print, though. She was still too shaken by that encounter with Leo. Why hadn't she put a stop to it before it had gone that far? Why had she let him get so close to her?

Because you couldn't stop him, she told herself with as much conviction as she could muster. He just sort of steamrollered over you. He's got a pretty powerful personality, although he tries to hide it under all that lazy charm. People like that always get their own way.

Ellie's nerves jumped edgily. She didn't like to think of Leo getting his own way; it conjured up pictures that were highly disturbing.

You've got to forget about him, she lectured herself. Anyway, you've probably seen the last of him now. He got what he came for—one more kiss. With luck, that should satisfy him.

Only she had the feeling that it took a lot more than just a kiss to satisfy Leo Copeland. He radiated sexual energy. A man like that would want a whole lot more than kisses from a woman.

Ellie sighed, turned the page of the newspaper, stared at the lines of black print, but couldn't seem to take any of it in. It might as well have been printed in a foreign language. Then she stared at it with some exasperation. It *was* in a foreign language.

She tossed it to one side, and instead picked up a brochure that gave information about places to visit in Cairo. On the cover was a photograph of the Pyramids, which immediately conjured up a picture of Leo in that absurd Egyptian guide's costume. Except that it had really rather suited him, murmured a small voice inside her head.

Oh, shut up! Ellie muttered in annoyance. She turned the page. She had definitely had enough of the Pyramids!

The next colour photograph was of the Egyptian Museum, though—the place where she had first met Leo.

It's a conspiracy! she decided crossly, and threw the brochure on top of the newspaper.

After that, she simply sat and stared at the walls. It was boring, but it was one way of keeping Leo Copeland out of her head.

When she heard the sound of Miss Mason's voice outside, Ellie sighed with relief. This was going to be one of the few times she would actually be pleased to see her! She hadn't expected her back so soon, though. Miss Mason must have cut short the visit to the museum and returned early, for some reason.

Ellie left the lounge, and found Miss Mason and the group of girls standing in the reception area.

'Ah, there you are, Miss Mitchell,' said Miss Mason with a small frown. 'Are you feeling better?'

'Yes, thank you,' replied Ellie, although that wasn't strictly the truth. In fact, she couldn't remember when she had last had such a disturbing afternoon. 'I didn't think you'd be back this soon,' she added.

'Sharon felt faint,' Miss Mason said with some annoyance. 'Since I had to cope with the entire group on my own, thanks to your indisposition, I thought it best to bring the girls back to the hotel.'

Ellie somehow stifled a grin. Sharon certainly knew how to cut short the endless museum visits!

'I've sent Sharon up to her room to lie down,' Miss Mason went on. 'The rest of you girls,' she added, turning to face them, 'I want you to go into the lounge and write some notes on what we've seen today.'

A suppressed groan went up, but no one had the nerve to argue with Miss Mason. The girls trooped half-heartedly into the lounge, settled themselves into chairs and took out their notebooks, while Miss Mason turned back to Ellie.

'I seem to have misplaced my guidebook, Miss Mitchell. I believe I may have left it at the museum. I'd like to borrow yours, if it isn't inconvenient. I want to look up a couple of things before we leave tomorrow.'

Ellie had actually forgotten that this was their last day in Cairo. In the morning they would be setting off down the Nile to Luxor, on the next stage of their trip.

Leaving Leo Copeland behind, she realised with a silent sigh of relief. No more charades, no more tension, no glancing over her shoulder all the time.

No more kisses, added that small voice that kept saying things she definitely didn't want to hear.

'Miss Mitchell?' prompted Miss Mason curtly. 'Did you hear what I said?'

'Oh—yes,' Ellie said quickly. 'You want to borrow my guidebook. I'll get it for you—it's up in my room.'

'I'll come up with you,' Miss Mason decided. 'I'll collect the book, then go and freshen up. It's very tiring taking a group of girls around this city on your own,' she added meaningfully.

'Yes—I'm sorry about that,' Ellie said guiltily. 'And I'm sure it won't happen again. I feel much better now. I'm certain I'll be able to manage the rest of the trip without any problems.'

'I do hope so.' With that, Miss Mason headed towards the stairs, leaving Ellie to trail along behind her feeling ridiculously like a schoolgirl herself. And a severely chastised schoolgirl at that!

When the two of them reached Ellie's room, Miss Mason stood tapping her fingers together rather impatiently as Ellie fumbled around in her bag for the key. Then she remembered that she hadn't locked the door. And a second later she remembered *why* she hadn't locked it. It had been because Leo had still been on the other side!

A great jolt of alarm rocked her. What if he was still there? As she considered that awful prospect, she felt every trace of color drain right out of her face.

'Are you all right, Miss Mitchell?' Miss Mason enquired sharply. 'You've gone very pale.'

'Yes, I'm—I'm fine,' gulped Ellie. She definitely wasn't, though. And she thought her legs would probably give way completely if she opened that door and gave Miss Mason a clear view of Leo wandering around her room. Or, even worse, sitting comfortably on the edge of the bed!

'Er—perhaps you'd like to go and freshen up, and I'll bring the guidebook along to you later,' she suggested with a nervous flutter of her hands.

'I'd like the book right now,' Miss Mason said firmly.

Ellie tried frantically to think of a good excuse for keeping the door to her room very tightly shut. Since she couldn't think of one, though, she slowly fumbled for the door-handle. Her heart gave a hefty thump as she turned it; then it gradually began to settle down again as she pushed the door open and found the room inside was quite empty.

The pent-up breath whistled out of her lungs in a long sigh of relief.

'Come on in,' she said almost cheerfully. 'The book's over there, on the cupboard beside the bed.'

Miss Mason stood just inside the doorway as Ellie went over to fetch the book. She felt positively light-headed with relief, and knew her face had returned to its usual healthy colour.

'Please keep the book as long as you like,' she said, walking back to Miss Mason and handing it to her.

'I'll only need it for an hour or two——' began Miss Mason. Then she stopped talking, her attention diverted by the bathroom door, which had just begun to swing open.

Ellie stared nervously in the same direction. Perhaps it's just a draught from a window blowing the door open, she muttered hopefully to herself. Then a tall male figure appeared in the doorway, and that faint hope immediately spluttered and died.

Ellie closed her eyes. Oh, please, don't let this be happening! she prayed silently. But it was, of course, and there wasn't a single thing she could do about it.

Leo emerged from her bathroom looking like one of the ancient male gods. And the main reason he gave that impression was that he was very nearly naked!

Anyone who appreciated the male body would definitely have been impressed. Leo undressed was somehow even more mind-bogglingly perfect than Leo fully clothed. Ellie had the feeling that Miss Mason wouldn't appreciate the aesthetic beauty of Leo's torso, though, or the long, powerful line of his legs. She would only see an almost naked man—and, since he was coming out of Ellie's bathroom, there were a couple of inescapable conclusions that she would immediately draw.

Leo hitched the towel a little tighter around his waist. Ellie wanted to yell at him that it was too late for that. It didn't really matter now if the wretched towel fell right off! Miss Mason had already seen almost everything there was to see, and Ellie knew there was no way she was going to be able to talk her way out of this.

She shot a quick sideways glance at Miss Mason, and the set expression on those sharp features told her everything she needed to know. Miss Mason didn't have an understanding or a forgiving nature. And she didn't believe in giving people the benefit of the doubt—or a second chance.

Ellie glared hotly at Leo, who seemed quite unperturbed by the situation. His mouth curled into a lazy smile, and his shoulders lifted into a shrug that didn't quite manage to be apologetic.

'Sorry,' he said, with great charm. 'Bad timing.'

'On the contrary,' said Miss Mason crisply, 'this simply confirms the doubts that I've had for some time. Miss Mitchell, it was against my better judgement that I took you on and gave you a chance, but we were very short-staffed and I didn't have much choice. You're obviously not a suitable person to be employed at Merralwood School, though, and I would like you to consider yourself dismissed, as from this moment. And, considering your lack of moral standards, I believe you should think very carefully before applying for another job which involves you with young people. Come and see me later, and we shall discuss severance pay and the arrangements for your return to England.'

With that, she turned and walked stiffly out of the room, leaving a speechless Ellie alone with Leo Copeland.

CHAPTER FIVE

ELLIE'S gaze fixed hostilely on Leo. 'Well?' she said icily. 'Are you satisfied now? Is this what you wanted all along? To make me lose my job?'

'I didn't know you'd be bringing Miss Mason up to your room,' Leo pointed out.

'If you hadn't been here in the first place, it wouldn't have mattered *who* I brought up here.' Ellie's tone remained coldly controlled. 'And what exactly were you doing in my bathroom?'

'Having a shower, of course—I wanted to wash that dye off my skin. Then I heard voices, so I came out to see who it was.'

'Picking the smallest towel you could find to wrap round yourself,' she said, her eyes still chilly.

She didn't understand why she wasn't losing her temper. She could feel the anger boiling round inside her, but none of it showed on the surface. Her voice was cold, but calm. She almost felt as if she were in control of the situation—even though she knew perfectly well that she wasn't.

'I think the size of the towel is fairly irrelevant here,' Leo said drily. 'Even a square inch of bare flesh would have been enough to have offended Miss Mason's sensibilities. What she objected to was the fact that I was in your room at all. And I've already apologised for that.'

'Have you? I don't remember hearing any apology.'

He smiled disarmingly. 'Perhaps I meant to apologise, but forgot. Anyway, there's no real harm done.

You've lost a job that you never liked in the first place, and you shouldn't have any trouble getting another.'

Ellie couldn't believe she was hearing this. 'No harm done?' she echoed in a rising tone as the suppressed anger finally began to burst through the unnatural calmness that had enveloped her. *'No harm done?* You've interfered in my life, you've made me lose my job, and you've got the nerve to stand there and say you haven't done any harm?'

Not a single sign of regret showed on Leo's face. 'I believe it's the best thing that could have happened to you,' he stated firmly.

'The best thing that could have happened to me was that I never set eyes on you!' Ellie hissed at him malevolently, her temper at last catching fire and beginning to blaze. 'You're an arrogant, loathsome man! You pushed your way into my life, you pawed me around, and now you expect me to be grateful— *grateful,*' she almost screeched, 'because you've got me the sack! And why am I meant to be grateful? Because *you* think it'll be good for me. *You* think I'm not cut out to be a teacher. Well, let me tell you something, Mr Copeland. I wanted that job. I needed that job! Of course, you wouldn't understand that, because you don't have the slightest idea what my life's been like this last year. You're not even very interested, are you? You just like playing games with people; it's how you get your kicks!'

She finished there, partly because she had run out of breath and partly because she felt an ominous pressure behind her eyes. Ellie didn't lose her temper very often, but when she did it all too often ended in a flood of tears, and she *wasn't* going to cry in front of Leo Copeland.

Leo had stopped smiling now. Instead, his brows were drawing together in a darkening frown, and he moved rather restlessly over to the far side of the room.

'I think you're over-reacting, Ellie.'

'You think I'm over-reacting? I do apologise,' she said with grinding sarcasm. 'I really am sorry I'm not taking this as well as you thought I would. I suppose most people don't mind at all when you turn their lives upside-down!'

Leo moved again. 'All right, perhaps I got it wrong. If I did, then I'll try and find a way to make it up to you. Either way, we need to talk about this some more. But I think I'd better get dressed before we take this any further.'

'Oh, please don't bother on my account,' she said bitingly. 'I'm not like Miss Mason—you won't offend *my* sensibilities. You can stand around totally naked, if you like, and I definitely won't faint or scream.'

Leo gave a low growl. 'I still feel at a distinct disadvantage, standing around like this.'

'Good heavens,' said Ellie with mock astonishment, 'Leo Copeland at a disadvantage? That's got to be a first!'

He shifted position again and muttered something under his breath.

'I didn't quite catch that,' she informed him.

'You weren't meant to.' His eyes suddenly shone hotly. 'But if you really want to know, I was telling myself to cool down. This towel's pretty revealing, and you're beginning to get to me, Ellie. When you lose your temper, you come alive. You're starting to make me want you, and this definitely isn't a good time or place.'

His blunt words brought the colour rushing to her face. With an effort she fought it back. She wasn't going to let him throw her any further off balance. And she kept her gaze carefully averted from his near-naked body.

'If you're having problems, I suggest you use the shower again,' she said in a detached voice. 'And this time, turn it to cold!'

'I don't think I need to do that. Believe it or not, I do have some self-control.' There was a dry note in Leo's voice now. 'But I'll go and get dressed. Perhaps we'll both feel better when I've got some clothes on.'

'Right now, I can't think of anything that'll make me feel better,' Ellie replied, and this time she couldn't quite keep the bitterness out of her voice.

'Then, between us, we'll have to try and find something,' he said in an unexpectedly quiet voice.

He disappeared back into the bathroom, and Ellie was glad of the couple of minutes' respite. She found she was shaking slightly, and her head was beginning to ache.

This had really been a totally disastrous day. It had started when she had first set eyes on Leo at the Pyramids this morning; had gone from bad to worse when he had barged into her room and started kissing her; and now it had ended in this final catastrophe.

For a few moments, she wondered if it was worth going to Miss Mason and begging for her job back. Perhaps she could try and explain how much it meant to her. Explain that the situation this afternoon hadn't been nearly as bad as it had looked.

Then she sighed. She knew perfectly well it would be a waste of time. Miss Mason never changed her mind, once she had reached a decision. And she had definitely decided that she no longer wanted to employ Ellie Mitchell at Merralwood School.

So that was it. Her small piece of security had gone. She was adrift again, with no job, no income, no one to turn to.

The rush of temper that had kept her going through that confrontation with Leo began to drain away, leaving her feeling completely empty and deflated. She didn't know where to go from here. She suddenly felt very lost and alone, and horribly close to tears again.

When Leo came back into the room, he found her sitting on the edge of the bed and staring rather fixedly ahead of her. She didn't look like the same girl who had been spitting mad just minutes ago. She didn't even look particularly angry with him any more.

For some reason, that bothered him. Her anger had been perfectly natural—and quite justified, he had to admit. There wasn't anything natural about this tense silence, though. And there was a withdrawn look in her eyes that disturbed him.

'Have you got over the urge to throw something at me?' he asked her lightly.

Ellie looked up at him. 'It rather looks like it,' she said in a flat voice.

'And I've got over the desire to take you to bed,' Leo said easily. 'Although I can't guarantee that it won't come back again at some time in the future.'

'Even if it does, it won't be a problem. I won't be around for much longer.'

'Where are you going?'

'Back to England, of course.' Back on the dole, she thought drearily. And with not much chance of getting a job in the near future, because she would be willing to bet Miss Mason wouldn't provide her with a glowing reference!

'I could suggest an alternative,' said Leo after a short pause.

Ellie looked at him with cold eyes. 'Yes, I'm sure you could. But I don't want to hear any of your suggestions, thank you.'

He studied her thoughtfully for a few moments, then he gave a brief shake of his head.

'All right, we'll leave this for now. I'm beginning to get the message. As far as you're concerned, I've done enough damage for one day. You don't want me around right now.'

'How very perceptive of you! Goodbye, Mr Copeland,' she said pointedly.

'Leo,' he reminded her.

She didn't even answer. Leo shot one last glance at her averted head, and a small frown creased his face. Then he turned away from her and slowly left the room.

Ellie only began to relax when she heard the door close behind him. She hadn't been at all sure that he would really go. Yet, funnily enough, once he had gone she felt even more alone.

She twisted her fingers together wryly. She must be feeling low if she was willing to admit that having Leo around was better than having no one at all!

She sat there for a long time, not quite able to find the energy—or the incentive—to move. It was still hard to take it all in. This morning she had had a job, a regular salary, and some kind of security in her life. Now, just a few hours later, they had all disappeared. She was right back where she had started.

Since she didn't want anything to eat, she didn't go down for the evening meal. Later that evening, though, she forced herself to go and see Miss Mason. After a thoroughly unpleasant interview, she finally returned to her room. In her hand she held her return air ticket to England. The only trouble was, it was dated a week from now, when the school trip was scheduled to finish. She would have to ring the airport in the morning, to try and change it.

If the airline wouldn't swop it for an earlier flight, though, she would just have to stay on in Cairo for a few more days. To her surprise, Miss Mason had already made arrangements to cover that possibility. She had spoken to the hotel manager, who had agreed that Ellie could stay on at the hotel until it was time for her to return home.

Since there was nothing else she could do right now about the situation, she eventually undressed and went to bed. She lay for a while staring up at the ceiling, still trying to come to terms with everything that had happened. Then, although she hadn't expected to, she fell asleep and slept peacefully right through the night.

When she woke up in the morning she felt much better. Calmer, more in control, and determined not to let this get her down.

After breakfast she phoned the airport, and they confirmed what she had already suspected: she couldn't change the date of her flight. If she wanted to return to England straight away, she would have to buy a new ticket. She couldn't really afford to do that, and anyway, she certainly didn't want to waste so much money. She was going to need every penny of her meagre savings in the future, now that she didn't have a job. And a few more days in Cairo wouldn't be such a hardship.

She had been using the phone in the lobby. As she put down the receiver and turned away, she had to come to an abrupt halt to prevent herself bumping right into Leo Copeland, who was standing only inches behind her.

Ellie glared at him. 'Were you eavesdropping on my telephone conversation?' she demanded.

'Not exactly eavesdropping,' said Leo, with a smile that positively dripped charm. 'But I was standing so close that I couldn't help hearing what you said.'

Ellie's lips set into a thin line. That meant he knew she would be in Cairo for a few more days. Briefly, she considered changing her plans and splashing out on that ticket, after all. Then she straightened her shoulders. She wasn't going to throw away much-needed money just because of Leo Copeland!

'Have Miss Mason and all her pretty little school-girls left?' Leo went on. His smile became laced with pure mischief. 'That woman will be grey-haired by the time she returns home. Every red-blooded man in the country will be interested in her gorgeous group of girls. She'll have her work cut out getting the whole lot home with their virtue intact!'

'They're only fourteen,' Ellie said in a cutting voice. 'And, whatever impression they might give, they're not promiscuous. They certainly don't sleep around.'

'I hope not, at that age,' agreed Leo. 'But to Miss Mason, even a kiss is taboo. And nowadays a lot of fourteen-year-olds do like to kiss. So do a lot of adults,' he added thoughtfully.

Ellie didn't like the way he was looking at her mouth. It reminded her of——

No, she didn't even want to think of what it reminded her of, she decided hastily.

'What are you doing here?' she asked curtly.

'I've come to see you, of course,' Leo answered easily.

She had expected him to say that. And she realised that she wasn't at all surprised to see him. In fact, she would probably have been disappointed if he *hadn't* turned up.

That last thought definitely startled her. She glanced at him, afraid he might be able to read her mind. He was still looking at her, and she hastily dropped her gaze. She had the feeling that her eyes sometimes revealed far too much.

'Let's go and find somewhere quiet, where we can talk,' he suggested.

'Like my room?' retorted Ellie, with renewed tartness. 'No, thank you. When I'm with you, I like to be in a very public place.'

'We were on a public street when I kissed you,' he reminded her softly. 'That didn't stop me, though.'

She sighed silently. She supposed he had a point there. And perhaps this conversation *would* be better conducted in private. She could never be sure what Leo was going to say—or do! She definitely didn't want half the guests in the hotel looking on if he took it into his head to do something outrageous.

'All right, we'll go up to my room,' she said with great reluctance. 'Although I think I'm mad even to talk to you at all.'

'You don't really have much choice, do you?' said Leo with a grin. 'You've already found out how hard it is to get rid of me.'

That was certainly true! Anyway, Ellie wanted to get this conversation over and finished with. Then she could concentrate on getting her life into some kind of order again. It would be much easier to do that once she had got rid of Leo once and for all.

When they reached her room, she deliberately left the door ajar. Leo noticed it, and raised one eyebrow.

'You don't feel safe with me?'

'I shouldn't think any female under eighty feels safe with you!' she retorted acidly.

'Oh, most of them are perfectly safe,' he assured her. 'For instance, I never felt the slightest inclination to seduce Miss Mason.'

Just the very thought of it made Ellie suddenly want to giggle. And that in itself was extraordinary, because she never giggled. She hardly ever laughed.

Get control of yourself, she ordered herself sternly. There's really nothing in the least funny about this situation. And it would definitely be a mistake if you let Leo start to amuse you. There's always something rather irresistible about a man who can make you laugh.

She forced a very neutral expression on to her face, then she looked at him again.

'Let me guess why you're here. You've come to offer me a job.'

He grinned. 'Am I that obvious?'

'No, you're not. But it's the kind of thing that a man with a guilty conscience *would* do.'

'I don't feel particularly guilty,' he told her.

'Then you should! You had no right to do any of the things you've done these last couple of days.'

Leo looked unabashed. 'Do you really regret losing that job? And be honest, Ellie,' he warned.

'Yes, I do regret it,' she answered at once. 'I told you, I *needed* it.'

His tawny eyes rested on her reflectively. 'But you never explained why you needed it.'

'No, I didn't. And I don't intend to! I don't have to explain my private life to you.'

'You might feel better if you did.'

His casual suggestion threw her briefly off balance. For a few moments she found herself thinking how nice it would be if she *did* have someone she could talk to. Then she dismissed that idea. Most people weren't interested in listening to other people's problems. They simply listened politely and tried not to look too bored.

'Tell me about this job you're offering,' she said, deciding it was time to change the subject.

'You already know most of the details.'

'It's that old offer you made? You still want to photograph me?' Ellie instantly looked scathing. 'That isn't a proper job!'

'But you can earn good money for the next few days,' Leo replied. 'I told you, I'll pay top rates. And as well as that you'll get expenses.'

She wasn't in the least impressed. 'It's hardly permanent, though.'

'No, it isn't,' he agreed. 'But I've got good connections. If you like, I'll give you an introduction to a reputable modelling agency, once this assignment's over. I can't give any guarantees that they'll take you on, but they'll certainly interview you and give you an honest assessment of your chances of making it as a model.'

The whole thing sounded quite ridiculous to Ellie. 'I'm twenty-three,' she informed him. 'That's far too old to take up that sort of career, even if I had the looks.'

'Twenty-three is hardly over the hill,' Leo said with a brief smile. 'And, although you don't seem to want to believe it, you *do* have the looks. Better than that, though, you're photogenic. And that's the most important asset of all.'

'How do you know I'm photogenic? You only took those few snaps in the bazaar, and you gave *me* the negatives. You didn't even see them.'

'I didn't have to,' he said simply. 'I knew it as soon as I saw you through my camera lens.' He looked at her with a directness that rather unsettled her. 'Wouldn't you like to travel all over the world and make a lot of money?'

'I don't know.' It certainly didn't sound like her kind of lifestyle. 'Anyway, it's not worth thinking about it, since it isn't going to happen.'

'It certainly *won't* happen if you don't even have the guts to give it a try.'

His reply really annoyed her. Who did he think he was, walking into her life and lecturing her like this? Anyway, she knew her limitations. She was Ellie Mitchell, failed schoolteacher, currently unemployed—*not* the stuff that top models were made of!

Leo accurately read the expression on her face. 'Someone needs to make you believe in yourself,' he said more quietly.

'And you're volunteering for that job?' she retorted acidly.

'I'm volunteering to help you take the first few steps.'

'Because you feel you owe it to me?'

His eyes flashed briefly. 'Because I think this is something you'd be good at. And because I want you for my series of photographs. I'm certainly not offering you charity. That would hardly be fair to you, and it definitely wouldn't do me any good.' His gaze became more challenging. 'Scared to try something new, Ellie?'

'No!' she shot back, without even thinking what she was saying.

'Then what's holding you back?'

You, she wanted to say. I don't want to work with *you*. I don't know why, but I just don't want to do it. The very thought of it makes me uneasy.

And on top of that, of course, she *was* scared. She didn't think she could do it. All this talk of being a model—it was nonsense, really ridiculous. She had never dreamt of tackling anything like that.

That's no reason to turn down the opportunity now it's been offered to you, argued that inconvenient little voice inside her head.

And there was the prospect of earning some money, of course. Even if the photo sessions didn't work out—and she didn't think for one moment that they would—Leo would still have to pay her those top rates he had promised. And if she used her brains, she should be able to make them last much longer than necessary, which would cost him even more than he had estimated. Her eyes began to shine more brightly, in anticipation. It would certainly be one way of making him pay—quite literally—for making her lose her job!

'How much would I earn an hour?' she asked thoughtfully.

When he told her, it made her eyebrows shoot up in astonishment. 'That much?'

'You can phone any of the agencies in London, if you like,' he offered. 'They'll confirm that that's the going rate.'

'And how long will this series of photos take?'

'Several days,' he replied. 'And they'll involve quite a lot of travelling. Everything will be paid for, of course. Hotel bills, meals, any out-of-pocket expenses—— And if we need to stay on in Egypt for an extra couple of days, making you miss your flight back to England, then your ticket home will be paid for as well.'

'It seems a big budget just for a holiday brochure,' Ellie commented.

'These are going to be top-of-the-range holidays,' said Leo. His mouth relaxed into a smile. 'That's another way of saying that they'll be very expensive. The brochure has to sell those holidays, so it's going to be crammed with seductive photos of Egypt at its most exotic. Ancient temples, local colour, gorgeous sunsets over the Nile—you know the kind of thing.'

'And how do I fit into all this?' asked Ellie curiously.

His gaze narrowed with satisfaction as he realised that she was seriously beginning to consider his suggestion.

'I want you in almost all of the pictures,' he told her. 'Sometimes you'll be in the foreground, sometimes just a small figure in the background to give the photo some perspective.' His eyes gleamed slightly mockingly. 'Think of yourself as the "Spirit of Egypt". That'll be the theme behind the series of photos.'

Ellie gave a sceptical snort of laughter. 'The spirit of Egypt? *Me?*'

'Just keep a straight face and you'll be fine.'

She looked at him with fresh suspicion. 'Are you sure this whole thing isn't some elaborate practical joke?'

'You'll believe it's for real when I make you stand out in the hot sun for hours until I've got just the shot I want,' Leo assured her.

'The spirit of Egypt,' she muttered again. 'It really does sound quite ridiculous!'

'Take a good look in the mirror and you'll see it isn't ridiculous at all,' he said equably. 'I told you before, you've got just the type of looks that I want. A conventional beauty wouldn't be any good at all. But with your dark hair, dark eyes, and that slightly exotic cast to your face—perfect,' he murmured, his gaze sliding appreciatively over her features. Then his tawny eyes met hers head on. 'Will you do it?'

Half an hour ago Ellie would have said a straight and immediate 'no'. Now she was surprised to find that she was actually considering it. And not just considering it. Part of her actually wanted to try something new.

Getting involved in this is not a good idea, she warned herself. As well as the actual challenge of the job, it would mean travelling around Egypt with Leo. Can you cope with that?

Yes, she decided with such a burst of confidence that she almost believed it. And if it gets too much of a problem you can always walk out. You don't have to stay if he really starts to hassle you. And if it *does* work out, you can earn good money. That would be a far more useful way of spending your time than just sitting around in this hotel for the next few days.

Leo was watching her closely. 'You might even find it's fun,' he said persuasively, as he saw her starting to waver.

'I'm not much good at having fun.'

He began to smile, as if she had made a joke. Then he realised that her tone was perfectly serious.

'Then perhaps that's an even better reason to come and work for me,' he said softly.

Ellie got up and walked across the room. 'When would we have to start?' she asked at last.

'As soon as possible. In fact, this afternoon would be ideal. I've a fairly limited amount of time to get this assignment completed, and I've already wasted a couple of days.'

'Because of me?'

'In a way,' he agreed. 'I couldn't get started on this assignment without the right model. Although I don't consider any time spent with you as wasted,' he added, his eyes glinting.

She shot a dark look at him. 'If I agree to do these photos, then I want you to cut out all these personal remarks. This is going to be a strictly working relationship.'

'Of course,' he agreed, so promptly that Ellie flashed a sceptical glance at him.

Did she believe him? Of course not! She wasn't *that* naïve. But there was no reason why she shouldn't take this job on her own terms. And Leo would eventually find out that Ellie Mitchell might be unemployed, down on her luck and without anyone very much to turn to—but she still had a mind of her own, and she was beginning to discover how to use it!

As Leo had threatened, he put her to work that same afternoon. She went down to the lobby at two o'clock, as instructed, and found him already prowling up and down, waiting for her. He took one look at her and immediately shook his head.

'That's no good. Not the look I want at all. Have you got any jeans?'

'No. Only some cotton trousers.'

'Then I suppose they'll have to do. Wear a loose shirt over them. White, if you can manage it. We can pick up some accessories on the way.'

Grumbling under her breath, Ellie went back upstairs to change. She had the feeling that she was about to see another side of Leo—the professional, dictatorial side, which came right to the fore when he was working.

A few minutes later she returned to the lobby, dressed as he had instructed. He ran a critical eye over her, then nodded.

'I suppose that'll have to do. I'll take you shopping tomorrow, to get the clothes we'll need for the later shots.'

He turned round and headed towards the door, and Ellie almost had to run to keep up with him.

'Where are we going?' she asked a little breathlessly.

'Back to the Pyramids.'

She stopped dead. 'What on earth are we going there for?'

Leo also came to a halt and looked at her with raised eyebrows. 'I'd have thought that was fairly obvious. When people pick up a brochure about Egypt, what's the first thing they expect to see?'

'The Pyramids,' Ellie said a little gloomily.

'Right. So let's try and take the kind of shots that'll make hordes of tourists want to rush to Egypt and see them in person.'

'OK,' she agreed, although without much enthusiasm, and began to turn in the direction of the bus station.

'Forget the bus,' said Leo. 'I've got a taxi waiting.'

Ellie brightened up a little at that. She hadn't been looking forward to the long, hot bus journey.

As she clambered into the taxi beside him, she gave him an enquiring glance.

'Does this all go on expenses?'

He hesitated for just an instant before nodding.

'You must be good at your job,' she went on. 'They seem to give you just about anything you want, as long as you bring back the right pictures.'

'Yes, I'm good at my job,' he agreed. Something in his tone discouraged any more questions, but that didn't bother Ellie. She had already decided she wasn't going to ask him anything else. She didn't want to show too much interest in him, or he might get the wrong impression!

She turned away from him and glanced out of the window. Then she frowned. She might not know her way around Cairo too well, but even she could figure out that they weren't heading in the direction of the Pyramids.

'Where are we going?' she asked a little nervously.

Leo shot a relaxed grin at her. 'Don't worry—this wasn't all an elaborate ruse to get you away from the hotel and then sell you off to white slave traders! We're going to the bazaar first, that's all. I told you, I want to pick up some accessories.'

Ellie swallowed more audibly than she had meant to. 'I certainly didn't think you were abducting me,' she denied stiffly. 'I'm not that naïve.'

His eyebrows rose lazily. 'No? Well, perhaps not,' he conceded. 'But I certainly don't think you're very experienced in a lot of things, Ellie.'

She opened her mouth, ready to argue with him, but then closed it again. She might not be totally innocent, but she was quite certain that Leo was streets ahead of her when it came to the kind of experience that he was talking about!

'We're almost at the bazaar,' she said a few moments later, determined to divert his attention.

'I know,' he agreed. He told the taxi-driver to stop, then opened the door. 'Wait here,' he told Ellie. 'I'll only be a few minutes.'

He was as good as his word. She didn't even have time to feel nervous about sitting alone in a taxi in the middle of Cairo. Leo slid back into the seat beside her, told the driver to take them straight to the Pyramids, then tossed a couple of items on to Ellie's lap.

She picked up a pair of earrings which were quite unlike the tiny, almost unnoticeable gold studs she usually wore. These were a cascade of sparkling gold teardrops, which chimed softly and musically against each other as they moved.

The other thing he had given her was a brightly patterned scarf in vivid shades of blue and gold.

'Tie it loosely round your waist,' he told her. 'I want a contrasting splash of colour against your white shirt and trousers.'

'I'll look like a gypsy,' she said, wrinkling her nose.

'There's nothing wrong with that. In fact, it's the impression I'm going for. Someone who's footloose, with no ties. Someone who's free to wander around wherever and whenever she pleases.'

Ellie was about to tell him she couldn't pretend to be someone like that. Then she stopped. She *didn't* have any ties. And now Leo had made her lose her job, she *could* go wherever she liked—at least, until the money ran out!

It was a rather startling thought, and she sat in silence for a while, trying to get used to it. The only restrictions on her life were the ones that she put there. If she wanted to, she could break loose and do any-thing—*anything*—she felt like.

She was still mulling over that extraordinary idea when they finally reached the Pyramids. It was only Leo opening the taxi door and hauling her out that finally brought her back to the present.

It was late in the afternoon now, and the dazzling midday sun had softened to a glowing gold.

Leo nodded in satisfaction. 'The light's just right. Let's get on with it before it starts to fade.'

Ellie stood around rather awkwardly. 'What exactly do you want me to do?'

'Just wander around looking at the site,' he instructed, taking one of his cameras out of the bag slung over his shoulder. 'And try to take no notice of me. Pretend I'm not here.'

Which definitely wouldn't be easy! Ellie told herself with a grimace.

'Shouldn't I be posing?' she asked him, as they made their way towards the Great Pyramid.

'That's exactly what I *don't* want you to do,' he told her. 'I want you to look as if you've wandered into the shot quite by accident.'

Well, that shouldn't be too difficult, Ellie decided. She felt as if this whole rather bizarre situation was one enormous accident!

She spent the next hour wandering around the site, with Leo only giving occasional instructions on which direction he wanted her to take. She could hear the camera clicking away, and was very conscious of it at first. She knew she was walking stiffly and had a rather fixed expression on her face. Gradually, though, she started to relax, and even began to forget that these photographs would be used commercially, and weren't just holiday snapshots.

'Good,' murmured Leo now and then, which surprised her because it meant he must be getting the pictures he wanted. She had expected this first session to be fairly disastrous, with her getting everything absolutely wrong and Leo yelling at her all the time. Instead he seemed very relaxed about the whole thing, which put her in a much better frame of mind, and he hadn't raised his voice to her once.

'That's about it,' he told her as they arrived back at the Great Pyramid. 'There should be a couple of shots there that I can use.'

Ellie's eyebrows shot up. 'Only a couple? But I could hear the camera clicking all the time. You must have taken hundreds!'

'Quite a few,' he admitted. 'But it's always like that. Most of them will be all right, but nothing special. With luck, though, two or three will be just what I was looking for.'

'What do we do now?' she asked, aware of an unexpected sense of anticlimax. 'Go back to Cairo?'

'Since we're here and we've got some free time, how about climbing the Pyramid?' suggested Leo. 'The view from the top's really something.'

'But it isn't allowed,' Ellie reminded him a little primly.

'Things that aren't allowed are usually more fun than things that *are* allowed,' he told her with an amused smile. 'And I want to see that view one more time. Coming with me?' he challenged her.

She meant to say no, but didn't. Quite suddenly, the prospect of doing something forbidden excited her. She knew it was a dangerous way to feel—especially if Leo was involved in any way—but she decided not to think about that right now. Instead, a new and slightly reckless light blazed in her dark eyes.

'Yes,' she said boldly. 'Yes, I'm coming.'

Leo's own eyes glowed with approval. 'Follow me, then—but be careful,' he warned. 'It's quite a climb, and some of the footholds are rather precarious.'

Ellie soon found out that was something of an understatement! She wasn't going to back out now, though. Puffing breathlessly, she clambered along in his wake, noting where he placed his hands and feet and carefully using the same holds.

Although the sun was beginning to slide down in the sky, the heat was still fierce and she could feel her clothes sticking to her damp skin. Now and then Leo stopped and helped her over a particularly steep part, his hands firmly gripping her wrists and hauling her up. Then, nearly half an hour after they had set out, they reached the top.

Ellie was still wheezing hard, although Leo seemed scarcely out of breath. When she had recovered from the climb, though, she lifted her head—then caught her breath.

Cairo and the surrounding desert were spread out all around them, and the view was breathtaking. It was lit by the golden glow of the sinking sun, and the faint shimmer of heat that rose from the baked ground gave everything a faintly unreal quality.

'Worth the climb?' Leo asked softly.

'Oh, yes!' she breathed. 'It's like having the whole world spread out at your feet.'

'Then you're glad you broke the rules for once?'

'Perhaps I should do it more often,' she said with a smile. 'I'm really enjoying this.'

He didn't smile back at her, though. Instead he looked at her with an expression that was hard to read.

'You really *don't* have much fun in your life, do you?' he said at last.

'Not a lot,' said Ellie absently, only half listening to what he was saying. She was still gazing at the sun-soaked scene stretched out in front of her.

'I've already begun to do something about that,' he said slowly. 'But perhaps there's even more I could do.'

Ellie heard his words, but didn't really take them in. And it was only much later that she remembered what he had said, and realised she should have taken it as a warning.

CHAPTER SIX

BY THE time they arrived back in Cairo, Ellie was nearly dead on her feet. The strains and tensions of the day, together with the physical effort required to climb up and down the Great Pyramid, had just about knocked her out.

As they went into the lobby, she turned to Leo and didn't quite manage to stifle a huge yawn.

'What's the programme for tomorrow?' she asked.

'I'll collect you around nine, then we'll do the rounds of some of the more picturesque mosques, and finish up in the bazaar. We should end up with some pictures of two very contrasting sides of Cairo.'

'Sounds fine,' she mumbled, having to make an effort even to take it in. There were really only two things she was interested in right now—a hot shower, and then a long nap before dinner.

She said goodbye to Leo, then trailed wearily up to her room. Her legs ached, her eyes were drooping sleepily, and yet she was aware of a strange sense of exhilaration. It had been a day quite unlike any other she could remember. A day when she had tried new things, and found they weren't impossible.

She fell asleep as soon as her head hit the pillow. Her skin and hair were still damp from her shower, but both had dried off by the time she eventually opened her eyes again.

A glance at the clock told her she had slept for nearly two hours. Ellie gave a groan. She had only meant to doze for half an hour! If she didn't get down to the dining-room in five minutes flat, she would be too late for the evening meal.

She managed to make it just in time, but felt rather self-conscious sitting there on her own. She ate fairly quickly, and, when she had finished her meal, decided to have an early night. Despite the nap before dinner, she still felt fairly knocked out.

She went up to her room and started to open the door; then she stopped for a moment. A tall figure at the end of the rather dimly lit corridor had caught her attention. It looked like——

No, it couldn't possibly be, she told herself with a shake of her head. It was just a trick of the light.

The figure came nearer, and a frown gathered on her face as she saw it more clearly.

It *was*! No one else had quite that shade of hair or those familiar tawny eyes.

Leo smiled at her engagingly. 'I missed you at dinner—I caught the early sitting. You must have come down later.'

'Never mind about dinner!' Ellie retorted. 'What are you doing here?'

'I've changed hotels,' he told her calmly. 'I thought it would be much more convenient if we were both staying under the same roof.'

'Convenient for whom?' she challenged suspiciously.

'For both of us, of course,' he replied smoothly. 'I won't have to spend hours trying to get through to you on the phone every time I want to make some alteration to our working arrangements.'

'And how is it convenient for *me*?' she demanded.

'Well—I'm close by, if you need me,' he answered with a grin.

'I won't need you,' Ellie said promptly.

Leo's eyes changed a fraction. 'Everyone needs someone at some time.'

'Not me! I've learnt——' Just in time, she stopped herself. She had been about to say she had learnt to do without other people, but she didn't want Leo to know about her private life. She never told people, if she could possibly avoid it. She hated to see the pity in their eyes. Even at school she had always pretended her parents were still alive. She hadn't wanted anyone to know she was an orphan.

Leo was looking at her curiously now. 'What have you learnt, Ellie?' he asked softly.

'Nothing,' she mumbled. She groped for the door-handle. Suddenly she didn't want to talk to Leo any more. She was tired and she had begun to feel vulnerable, and both those things put her at a disadvantage. She might end up saying a whole lot more than she wanted to.

She managed to get the door open and thankfully hurried inside. Before she had a chance to shut it, though, Leo followed her in. She turned round to glare at him, determined to order him to leave. Then something in his eyes made her stop. Instead, she looked at him with some uncertainty.

'What is it?' she asked at last.

'I don't know,' he replied slowly. 'Just now and then, when I'm with you, I get the feeling that——'

'That what?' Ellie asked, in a slightly croaky voice.

'That I'm not quite in control of things.' A dry smile touched the corners of his mouth. 'It's a new experience for me. And I'm not altogether sure how to handle it.'

Neither of them had made any effort to switch on the light. The room was almost in darkness, with just a thin wedge of light shining in from the corridor outside. Ellie realised that Leo only had to push the door shut completely and there would be no light at all.

Really, you ought to be doing something about this, she told herself shakily. In fact, you should never have let him follow you in. Standing in a dark room having this odd conversation with him is definitely *not* a good idea.

She didn't move, though, and she didn't say anything. And Leo remained uncharacteristically quiet as well.

'I'm not sure where we should go from here, Ellie,' he said at last. 'I mean, I know where I *want* to go,' he added wryly. 'But it's not turning out to be as simple as I thought it would be.'

'What's making it complicated?' she asked unsteadily.

'You are.'

'I don't understand.'

'I'm not sure that I do either,' Leo said slowly. 'But I'll try and show you what I mean...'

He bent his head and kissed her lightly, and Ellie knew it was time to back off, but she didn't actually do it. When the kiss was over, Leo raised his head again and looked at her consideringly. She could just make out his features in the dim light, and noted a hot flare in his eyes which she immediately recognised.

'You see?' he said, a slight catch in his voice. 'One brief kiss, and I want you.'

Ellie shifted uneasily. 'Then don't kiss me. That way it won't be a problem.'

'But I *like* having this sort of problem. And I can cope with it, as long as it doesn't go too far. The only trouble is, I don't think you share it.'

'Why should I?' she said defensively.

'Because it would be good for both of us,' he said a little huskily. 'And normally, I'd know exactly how to get you in the right mood. First, I'd kiss you like this——' His mouth found hers again, more insistently this time, his lips leaving an imprint that would take a long time to fade, and his tongue gently probing until she allowed it entry into the soft inner warmth of her mouth. 'Then I'd touch you,' he murmured, and his hands were moving even before he had finished speaking. 'I know how to touch in all the right places,' he told her without any arrogance, just confidence in his own ability to please. And Ellie would have found it hard to argue with him about that. His fingers slid over her skin with delicious expertise, and she felt the stirrings of a pleasure that threatened to escalate beyond anything that anyone had ever aroused in her before.

'But do you know the biggest turn-on of all?' enquired Leo softly. 'It's knowing that someone wants you. So I'd bring you closer—like this—and let you *feel* what you do to me.'

Ellie's heart was thumping very hard by now, and she couldn't quite believe she was being so compliant. Why was she letting him hold her so very close, with every inch of his aroused body seeming moulded against hers?

Perhaps it was because she couldn't actually seem to do anything about it. And he was right, it *was* a turn-on. It gave her an unexpected feeling of power, of exhilaration.

Then he released her, and disappointment immediately shot through her. It was underlined with a sense of relief, though, because she knew how easily this could have all got out of hand.

Not for the first time, Leo seemed to read her thoughts. 'You see why it's complicated?' he said softly. 'I could have pushed you, Ellie. And I could probably have got what I wanted, because I'm good at this. That isn't a vain boast, it's just a simple fact. With anyone else, I probably *would* have pushed it. I always enjoy sex, as long as my partner's willing.'

'Then—why did you stop?' Ellie whispered unsteadily.

'Because you're not ready for this. You don't want it enough—not yet. And I don't know why, but that would take any pleasure out of it for me. I'm not willing to settle for a night that we'd both enjoy, but regret as soon as the morning comes.'

She swallowed hard, her throat suddenly dry. 'What are you going to do, then?'

Even in the half-light, she could see the smile that crossed Leo's face. 'What am I going to do? I'm going to let you get a good night's sleep, so you'll look fresh-faced and bright-eyed for tomorrow's photo session. And *I'm* going to lie awake most of the night, telling myself I'm a damned fool for walking away from you like this,' he said drily.

'This is—well, it's going to make it rather hard to work together, isn't it?' Ellie said edgily.

'I don't see why. Not if we both make a real effort to get back to that working relationship that you were so insistent about earlier.' Leo began to back away from her. 'I think I'd better leave now before I'm tempted to change my mind. Goodnight, Ellie.'

'Goodnight,' she muttered under her breath, but he didn't hear it. He had already gone.

Ellie closed the door, but didn't turn on the light. For some reason, she preferred the darkness.

Perhaps it was because she didn't want to look in the mirror and see her own face, she thought rather shakily. She didn't think she wanted to see what was written there.

Very slowly she got undressed and climbed into bed. Contrary to Leo's prediction, though, she didn't sleep well. And she couldn't get rid of the unsettling feeling that the old Ellie was slowly disappearing. She was beginning to turn into someone that she didn't know very well.

Ellie wasn't at all eager to face Leo again in the morning. She didn't understand what had happened the night before, and she wasn't sure that she *wanted* to understand it. Her life had become confusing enough ever since he had stepped into it. Right now, she didn't need anything more to cope with.

She soon discovered that she needn't have worried about it. Leo had said last night that they should get back to a working relationship, and he seemed determined to stick to that decision. He was all cool efficiency this morning, with a heavy schedule planned for the day, and every intention of getting through it. It was almost as bad as being back with Miss Mason! Ellie thought more than once.

In fact, for the next couple of days Ellie hardly had a chance to sit down. First, Leo whizzed her in and out of dress shops, where he picked out the outfits he wanted her to wear over the next few days. Then the photo sessions began in earnest. Whatever Leo was like at other times, once he was behind the camera he became totally professional, issuing crisp instructions, knowing exactly what he wanted, and willing to spend all day getting the shot that he was looking for. And although he was staying in the same hotel, he didn't come near her room again. Ellie might have believed she had dreamt the whole episode if she hadn't so vividly remembered what his mouth and hands had felt like when they had touched her. No one had dreams quite as real as that!

On the morning of the fourth day, Leo announced that he wanted to take some shots of her just walking through the streets of Cairo. He wanted a series of pictures that would give a flavour of the city. Ellie thought that sounded simple enough, but soon discovered her mistake. Leo seemed willing to walk for miles, ignoring the heat, the noise and the crowds, in order to find the perfect background for his photos. And, to Ellie's amazement, he didn't once get lost, even though they wandered for what seemed like hours through a maze of back streets and alleyways. Yet she had to admit that it was fascinating. The area was stuffed with medieval mosques, bustling squares, donkeys, camels and cars, the pungent aromas of spices and exotic food, and the stronger smells of heat, dust and livestock.

By the end of the morning Ellie's head was whirling with all the vivid impressions that had been crammed into it, and her feet felt completely worn out. She finally managed to coax Leo into a restaurant, where she collapsed limply into a chair.

'You're a slave-driver!' she accused.

'I like to work hard,' he agreed comfortably. 'But I'm also good at relaxing.'

'There doesn't seem to have been much time for relaxation over the last few days,' Ellie said darkly.

'That's because I'm working to a schedule.'

She gave a groan. 'Don't mention schedules! It reminds me of Miss Mason.'

Leo looked at her thoughtfully. 'Since you've brought up the subject of Miss Mason—are you still sorry you lost that job?'

'Of course,' Ellie said at once. 'That job meant security. This might be fun, but it hardly counts as permanent employment.'

Then she was immediately annoyed with herself for admitting that she was finding this fun. She hadn't meant to let Leo know that. She gave a brief scowl, and warned herself to be more careful in future. It didn't seem a good idea to let this man know too much about her private thoughts and feelings.

'By the way, this is our last day in Cairo,' Leo told her casually. 'Did I tell you that?'

'No, you didn't. Where are we going from here?'

'Luxor. We're catching the sleeper at half-past seven this evening.'

'This evening?' she squeaked. 'Why didn't you tell me before? This is pretty short notice!'

'How much time do you need?' he asked with some amusement. 'You've got all afternoon to pack.'

'Well, yes—but . . .' Ellie's voice trailed away because she didn't want to tell him she wasn't worried about getting packed in time. It was the thought of leaving Cairo that was unsettling her. For some reason, she felt safe here. She had seen so much of the city that it was beginning to feel familiar. Now she was moving off to Luxor, a totally strange place—and with only Leo for company.

She felt vaguely uneasy all through the afternoon, but she still packed her bags, ready to leave that evening. You're earning good money, she reminded herself more than once. There's no point in walking out on all that extra cash just because your nerves feel a bit twitchy!

The only trouble was, she knew *why* they felt twitchy. It was because of Leo and his wretched kisses. How could a kiss be so hard to forget? she asked herself with some exasperation. Most of the kisses she had had during the past few years had been instantly forgettable. Even Steven, whom she had genuinely thought she had loved, hadn't made much of a physical impression on her. Now she could hardly remember what the touch of his lips had felt like. In fact, Steven himself was little more than a fading blur in her memory.

And this was the man she had so desperately wanted to marry, she reminded herself drily. The man who had made her feel almost suicidal when he had walked out on her.

Ellie began to realise just how much she had changed during the last year. She had come through the bad times, and they had actually made her stronger. Even the fits of depression were no longer something to fear. She had conquered them, and they wouldn't be back. She was still on her own, of course, but she was finally learning to live with that. She didn't like it, but she could cope with it. She was never going to go completely under again.

But she had the feeling that even more startling changes had taken place over the last few days. She didn't know how or why it had happened, but she seemed to have become a more confident person since she had met Leo. It was as if he had brought out a side of her nature that had always been hidden before. He seemed to see something in her that other people just didn't see, and she responded positively to it.

Ellie stared thoughtfully at her reflection. Then she gave a brief shake of her head. Stop being fanciful! she instructed herself. Leo's just a man and this is just a job. Don't try and take it any further or you're going to regret it!

She was ready to leave on time, lugging her suitcase down to the reception area, where Leo was waiting. Her case felt heavier than usual because it contained the clothes which he wanted her to wear for the photo sessions in Luxor.

'Want me to carry it for you?' he offered.

'Thanks, but I can manage,' she replied. Then she looked pointedly at his own two bulging cases. 'Anyway, I should think you'll only just about be able to carry your own. Did you bring your entire wardrobe with you?'

'No,' Leo replied comfortably. 'But I always tote around a lot of photographic equipment. I never know quite what I'm going to need, so I play safe and bring as much as I can.' He picked up the cases without any difficulty. 'Let's get going, or we'll miss the train.'

The station seemed a crowded, confusing place to Ellie, but, as usual, Leo appeared to know exactly where to go. He strode confidently on ahead, with Ellie trudging along behind him, certain that he wouldn't get lost.

He arrived in the right place at the right time, of course. The train was waiting for them, and Ellie thankfully scrambled aboard. She knew she would never have tackled a journey like this on her own— her new-found confidence didn't stretch that far! With Leo to steer her through any difficulties, though, she found she was actually beginning to look forward to it.

He opened the door of one of the compartments and gently shunted her inside.

'This is it,' he told her.

She looked round in some surprise. It was a lot more comfortable than she had expected. It even had a small clothes closet, and a sink with hot and cold running water.

She dumped her case on the floor and smiled at him. 'This is fine—almost luxurious! Where's your compartment? Next to this one?'

'We're sharing this compartment,' he told her in a relaxed tone. 'It sleeps two people. My expenses aren't so unlimited that I can afford a separate compartment for each of us.'

All along, Ellie had had the feeling that there was going to be a catch to this situation. It had all been going too well. She didn't usually have that sort of luck. Something always turned up to ruin things.

She picked up her case. 'I'm not sharing a compartment with anyone,' she said firmly. 'And I think you knew that all along, or you'd have told me about this arrangement before we set out.'

'I never even gave it a thought,' Leo replied frankly. 'I've shared compartments before, sometimes with people I don't even know, because it's a way of splitting the cost. Don't be childish about this, Ellie. It's just a very practical travelling arrangement, that's all.'

She scowled at him. He was managing to make the whole thing sound so very plausible! But she was almost certain—no, she *knew*—that he had some ulterior motive.

'You should have told me about this before we set out,' she insisted.

'I had too many other things to do. Anyway, it never occurred to me that you were so prudish.'

Ellie wondered if he had used that word on purpose, just to rattle her. And the annoying thing was that it did. Old maids were prudish. Silly, nervous young girls were prudish. He probably knew perfectly well that she didn't want to be put into either of those categories.

'I still don't like it,' she muttered at last.

Leo finally began to lose patience. 'Then sleep in the corridor. You'll be pretty uncomfortable, but at least you won't have to worry about me pouncing on you in the night!'

'There's another alternative,' she said defiantly. 'I could forget about this trip, and go back to the hotel.'

Just then, though, the train made a clanking sound and began to pull out of the station.

'Too late,' Leo informed her, his eyes momentarily gleaming.

'I could get off at the next station.'

'This is an express train,' he told her. 'It doesn't stop until it gets to Luxor.'

Ellie rather sulkily sat down. She hated to admit it, but it looked as if there wasn't any way out of this situation. Short of taking up Leo's suggestion that she should spend the entire night in the corridor— and she certainly didn't intend to do that—she was going to have to share this compartment with him.

Leo looked very relaxed again now. As well he might! she told herself with a silent snort. Men were always pleased with themselves when they got their own way!

'You'll be perfectly safe,' he assured her, his voice betraying his amusement. 'All our meals will be served here, in the compartment, so there'll be waiters in and out, bringing dinner and breakfast. And, even when we *are* on our own, there isn't much I could get up to in a confined space like this. The bunks are fairly cramped,' he pointed out. 'Not much room to do anything except sleep.'

Ellie was sure he could find a way if he wanted to, though. Yet *did* he want to? That was the question she couldn't quite figure out. At the beginning of the week she would have said a very definite yes. His attitude certainly seemed to have changed since they had settled down to some serious work, though.

Perhaps he had never been particularly interested in the first place, she told herself. Maybe he had just set out to flatter her, in order to get her to agree to the photo sessions.

She found she didn't like that idea, which was silly really, since it should have made her feel a lot safer. In the end, she decided to stop thinking about it altogether. Somehow she would get through tonight. And in the future she would concentrate on her work and stop worrying about what was going on inside Leo Copeland's head.

As Leo had promised, dinner was brought to their compartment. A little earlier, Ellie hadn't felt in the least hungry. As soon as the food was placed in front of her, though, she discovered she had got her appetite back and ate every last mouthful.

But when the plates had been cleared away some of her original unease began to return. That was it until morning, when the waiter would bring their breakfast. That left an awful lot of long, dark hours to get through!

'Starting to feel nervous again?' enquired Leo, his eyes glinting a little wickedly.

'Certainly not,' replied Ellie with some annoyance, wishing he didn't find it quite so easy to work out what she was thinking.

'I've already told you that these bunks are too cramped for a serious attempt at seduction. I like a lot of space—room to move around.' His voice had dropped to a low, deliberate purr, and Ellie knew he was having fun, baiting her. Well, she wasn't going to respond to it! She would simply ignore him, and go to bed.

Then she realised that wasn't going to be as easy as it sounded. She would have to wash in front of him; *undress* in front of him.

She cleared her throat. 'Er—I expect there's a lounge car, if you want to go and stretch your legs. You might even be able to get a drink.'

'I don't need alcohol to help me sleep,' Leo said lazily. 'And I don't particularly want to stretch my legs.'

Ellie shot a fierce glare at him. She was quite sure he *knew* she was trying to get rid of him while she got ready for bed. And he had obviously made up his mind that he was going to stay exactly where he was.

Well, two could play at that game! she decided grimly. She would sit here all night, if necessary. She definitely wasn't going to *ask* him to leave. She could just imagine how he would laugh at her if she did that.

He was watching her again now, which only added to her annoyance. He seemed to spend an awful lot of his time just staring at her! What did he find so interesting about her very ordinary eyes, nose and mouth?

'I still can't quite figure you out,' he said at last, settling back into a relaxed position and still studying her.

'Why do you even want to?' she shot back at once, rather defensively.

'I don't really know,' he admitted, with unexpected frankness. 'Except that I enjoy solving mysteries.'

'There's nothing very mysterious about me. You're just talking rubbish.'

Leo shrugged. 'Maybe. But do you realise that I really don't know much more about you than when we first met?'

'And you want me to tell you my life story, just to satisfy your curiosity?' she retorted.

'No,' he replied easily. 'I think it would be more fun to get to know you slowly. But it sometimes bothers me that I don't even seem to be making a start.'

Ellie had the feeling that they were shifting on to dangerous ground here, and she didn't like it. She didn't want him probing into her past because she knew she would absolutely hate it when he started feeling sorry for her. And he *would* start feeling sorry; people always did. A pitying look crept into their eyes as soon as they found out she had no family, no one close to her, and it always made her cringe.

'I could say the same thing about you,' she said crisply. 'I know your name, and the fact that you're a professional photographer, and that's about it.'

'What else do you want to know?' he invited. 'Ask whatever questions you like. I don't mind.'

Ellie hadn't been expecting that sort of open response. For a few moments she didn't know quite what to say. Then she decided she might as well take up his offer. At least it would stop him asking a lot of awkward questions about *her*.

'How did you get into photography?' she said at last, deciding that would be a fairly safe question.

'Through my father. It's always been a great passion of his. He's got a dark-room that most photographers would give their right arm for, and a fantastic collection of cameras.'

'Is he a professional, like you?'

Leo seemed to hesitate for an instant. 'No,' he said at length. 'He's a banker. Or rather, he was. He's retired now, which means he can spend as much time as he likes out with his camera. It drives my mother crazy—she's always complaining that she never sees him. What does your father do?'

The question, tacked so smoothly on to the end, caught her off balance.

'He's—he—he's retired as well,' she muttered at last. It was the old lie, the one she had always trotted out at school and college when the question of parents came up. Her father was in poor health, she told them, so her parents had gone to live in the peace and quiet of the countryside. That was why she lived with her grandparents, although her parents kept in touch, of course, they rang her every couple of days and she went to stay with them during the holidays.

Silly to keep up that pathetic pretence after all this time. She had done it for so long, though, that she couldn't seem to stop.

Leo's eyes narrowed speculatively, as if he knew perfectly well she wasn't telling the truth. To her relief, though, he didn't ask any more questions. Instead he changed the subject, and began to explain the schedule he had roughed out for the couple of days they would be spending in Luxor.

A short while later he levered himself to his feet. 'I'm going to bed,' he announced. 'Do you want the top or the bottom bunk?'

Ellie tried to decide if she would feel safer with Leo above or below her. In the end, she decided that it really wouldn't make the slightest difference. Either way, she wasn't going to sleep easily tonight.

'The bottom bunk,' she answered at last. 'If that's all right with you.'

'I never mind too much where I sleep,' he replied easily. 'Although, believe it or not, I am rather more particular about who I sleep *with*.'

Before Ellie had time to get nervous about that last remark, he slid off his shirt and began to run some water in the small sink. He washed with the neat efficiency of someone who was used to the cramped conditions encountered during long-distance travel. Then he turned back to Ellie as he towelled himself dry.

'I never bother with pyjamas when I'm on the move like this—I just sleep in my underpants. If it's going to embarrass you, you'd better look the other way.

His suggestion was accompanied with a wide grin which, for some reason, made her bristle. She wished she had the nerve to sit and coolly watch him while he undressed! Instead, though, she stiffly turned her head and stared out into the blackness of the night until she heard the top bunk creak as Leo climbed into it.

She ran some water for herself, but didn't wash nearly as thoroughly as Leo, since she removed hardly any clothes. She promised herself a long, hot shower as soon as they arrived at the hotel in Luxor, then set about trying to solve the problem of how to get undressed without giving Leo an excellent view of the whole procedure.

She finally managed it by sitting crouched on her bunk, wriggling awkwardly out of her clothes and into her thin cotton nightdress. With a sigh of relief, she slid under the light coverings and closed her eyes.

'Sleep well, Ellie,' came Leo's faintly amused comment from just above her.

She had every intention of doing just that. It wasn't easy, though, with the rattling of the train and the constant movement.

Ellie knew it wasn't just the train that was keeping her awake, though. Leo hadn't said another word, and yet she was acutely aware of him, such a short distance away from her.

This situation was just too—well, too *intimate*, she told herself with a dark frown. Eating together, washing and getting undressed in the same confined space, lying here and listening to the quiet sound of his breathing. It was almost like being an old married couple!

And, although Leo hadn't stirred or spoken, she somehow knew that he was awake as well. That didn't help her peace of mind. She had the disturbing feeling that he was lying there, waiting for her to say something, or even to make a move.

Well, she wasn't going to do either of those things! she assured herself staunchly. Instead, she closed her eyes and concentrated fiercely on forgetting about Leo and going to sleep. She didn't manage it for another couple of hours, though. And she had the feeling that he slept as little as she did that night.

CHAPTER SEVEN

THE train finally rattled into the station at Luxor at half-past seven the next morning. By then Ellie was up and dressed, and had eaten breakfast.

When she had first woken up, she had found she had the compartment to herself. Taking advantage of Leo's absence, she had hurriedly stripped down and had a thorough wash. She needn't have rushed, though, because he didn't return to the compartment for another half-hour.

As usual, he was comfortably dressed in jeans and a loose cotton shirt. His tawny gold hair glinted brightly in the early morning sunshine that poured through the window, and Ellie was suddenly struck by the fact that this was a man whom a lot of women would like to spend the night with.

Well, she had. And nothing had happened! She couldn't quite believe it, but she supposed she just ought to be grateful. So why did she actually feel slightly piqued?

She was tired, that was all, she told herself rather crossly. She hadn't slept well—which was one more thing to blame on Leo—and that always made her feel out of sorts.

Luxor turned out to be much smaller than Cairo, although no less crowded and bustling. It was a mixture of exotic history and sheer commercialism, a city striving to cope with the hordes of tourists that descended on it, and managing very well.

From the moment that Ellie first set eyes on it, she loved it. Luxor was full of contrasts; grand architecture and mud-brick tenements, horse-drawn carriages and noisy taxis, luxury cruise ships moored alongside feluccas, the ancient boats of the Nile with their big triangular sails.

And, of course, there was the river itself. Luxor was set right on the banks of the Nile, which swarmed with life and seemed to change character with every slight alteration of the light.

Their taxi took them along the Corniche Road, where the main string of hotels were situated. Some were modern and soulless, but, to Ellie's delight, the taxi eventually pulled up outside a hotel built of a pale golden stone which glowed in the sunlight. Ornate balconies perched underneath the shuttered windows, and slim colonnades framed the main entrance.

'Like it?' asked Leo.

'It's perfect!' she breathed.

'I've booked rooms at the front of the hotel, so you should have a good view of the Nile from your window,' he went on. 'But don't spend all morning looking at the view! I want to go to the Valley of the Kings to photograph the tombs of the Pharaohs.'

Ellie groaned. 'We're going to start work straight away?'

'Of course. We'll only be here for a couple of days, and I've got a lot to fit into that time. Oh, and wear the green outfit. That should be perfect for the shots I want today.'

She dragged her gaze away from the fascinating sights, and reminded herself that she was being paid to model for Leo's photographs. She wasn't here on holiday.

'I'll be ready in half an hour,' she promised. Thirty minutes later, she had unpacked, had a quick shower and wriggled into the jewel-bright clothes that Leo had bought for her in Cairo. As always, she left her hair loose. Leo liked it simply drifting casually around her shoulders. Then she took a quick glance at her reflection.

Normally, she would never have worn anything in such a dazzling colour. Leo had picked an emerald-green blouse, worn over a loose casual skirt in the same shade, but bordered with gold. Ellie wasn't sure if she felt comfortable in these clothes or not. They certainly made her stand out from the crowd, and she wasn't used to that. She could see that they did great things for her colouring, though, throwing her black hair and dark eyes into vivid relief, and bringing out the golden glow of her skin as it tanned a shade deeper each day.

When she hurried downstairs to rejoin Leo, he seemed surprised to see her.

'Not many women really mean it when they say they'll be ready in half an hour!' he commented drily.

'Do I look all right?' she queried anxiously.

His expression changed and became less readable. 'As far as I'm concerned, you always look all right.'

His reply confused Ellie, who wasn't quite sure how to take it. And his eyes gave nothing away either. They were a particularly impenetrable shade this morning.

'Let's get going,' he added. 'The Valley of the Kings is on the far bank of the Nile. We'll have to catch the ferry across the river.'

Ellie was rather relieved to be on the move. She never felt particularly safe when Leo began to make personal remarks.

She enjoyed every moment of the trip across the river, even though the ferry was crowded with tourists. When she was with Leo, she seemed to be able to forget about the people jostling all around her.

The ferry finally arrived at the other side, and he turned to her with a faint grin. 'It's still quite some distance to the Valley of the Kings—too far to walk in this heat. Shall we take a taxi, rent a couple of bicycles, or do you fancy a donkey ride?'

Ellie looked at the patiently waiting donkeys, and promptly shook her head. 'They look worn out already, poor things. I'm not going to make them walk any further in this hot sun.'

Leo's eyebrows lifted gently. 'I told you once before that you were soft. And, if I remember rightly, you denied it.'

'I'm not soft,' she insisted stubbornly. 'I'm just not going to ride one of those animals.'

'That's OK by me,' he said amicably. 'A donkey isn't the easiest—or the most comfortable—way of getting around. And, if you don't mind, we'll pass on the bicycles as well. A lot of those machines look as if they'll collapse after the first couple of hundred yards. We'll take a taxi.'

They finally roared off in a noisy, rattling car. The land around here was dry and brown and dusty, in contrast to the green fields that flanked the banks of the Nile, irrigated by its waters. They were nearing the edge of the hot, barren desert that covered much of Egypt, and the heat was quite intense.

The taxi deposited them at the entrance to the Valley of the Kings, and the driver promised to wait for them.

Leo unslung his camera, then motioned to Ellie to walk on ahead.

'I want some general scenic shots,' he instructed. 'Just wander around, but keep your head up so I can get a good view of your face.'

It took him half an hour to get the pictures he wanted, and by then Ellie was just about ready to melt away in the heat. The midday sun was pounding down on them, brilliant and dazzling, making her eyes ache.

'I thought you preferred to take pictures in the early morning and late afternoon,' she complained.

'I do,' agreed Leo. 'But I wanted to take a few that were very bright and sharp. They'll contrast well with the more moody shots of the Nile that I'm going to take later.'

'Well, if we don't get out of this sun soon, I think I'm going to get heatstroke!'

'Let's head for one of the tombs, then. I'll try some interior shots.'

The entrance to the nearest tomb was little more than an opening cut into the hillside. It wasn't much cooler inside, but at least they were away from the blinding glare of the sun, and Ellie was grateful for that.

She scrambled along behind Leo as he made his way down the sloping corridor that led into the tomb, and reflected that a model's life wasn't exactly glamorous—at least, not when you worked for Leo! They eventually came to an antechamber, with walls decorated with paintings of animals, serpents and demons. Ellie waited patiently while Leo took some photos, then followed him again as he made his way even deeper into the tomb.

When they finally reached the burial chamber, she caught her breath. The ceiling had the body of a goddess painted right across it.

'According to myth, this particular goddess swallowed the sun each evening and then restored it the next morning,' Leo told her softly.

'Quite a feat!' said Ellie, still staring up admiringly at the painting. 'But she is beautiful.'

'I prefer to look at you.'

She hadn't been expecting him to say anything quite like that. She looked away from the ceiling, shifted uneasily, then glanced around. For the first time, she realised that they were alone in this tomb. There had been other tourists wandering around outside, but none of them seemed to have headed in this direction.

'I always seem to be crawling around inside ancient monuments with you,' she said with a rather feeble attempt at a smile. 'First the Great Pyramid, and now a Pharaoh's tomb.'

'Are you trying to change the subject, Ellie?'

'I can't even remember what the subject was,' she lied.

Leo raised his camera and took several careful shots of the ceiling. Then he replaced the camera in its case, leant back against the wall and let his gaze rest on her.

'I was telling you that I find you more interesting than all the wall paintings in the Valley of the Kings put together.'

'I'm not sure that's a compliment!' she responded, trying to turn the whole thing into a joke because she had a feeling this would be a lot easier to handle if she kept it on a strictly non-serious level.

'It was a compliment,' he confirmed in a level voice. His gaze flickered. 'Don't you like them?'

'Compliments? I don't really know. I don't get a lot of them.'

This time his eyebrows lifted extravagantly. 'Are you telling the truth?'

'Of course.' When he didn't say anything more, Ellie walked a little nervously over to the far side of the burial chamber. Then she turned and faced him again. 'Look, I'm not very good at these sort of games,' she said bluntly. 'I'd prefer it if you just came right out and told me what you want from me.'

'And if I do?'

'I'll tell you that you can't have it. We'll both know where we stand then, and that'll make things a lot easier. In fact, we might even be able to forget about it and get on with some work.'

'But what if I'm being serious about this?' Leo suggested, his gaze concentrating on her fully now.

Despite the stuffy heat inside the tomb, a series of small shivers skittered over her skin.

'I don't believe you are,' she said with far more conviction than she actually felt.

'Why not?'

'For the same reason that I don't believe you when you tell me I've got an exotic face. I *know* I look quite ordinary. Other people know it too. No one else has ever said anything like that to me.'

Leo's mouth relaxed into an unexpected smile. 'Are you accusing me of being short-sighted?'

'Of course not! I'm just saying——' Ellie stopped there, because she suddenly wasn't at all sure that she wanted to finish that particular sentence.

It didn't matter, though, because Leo finished it for her.

'You're saying I see you differently from everyone else?' he said quietly.

Ellie remembered those photos he had taken of her. The photos in which she hadn't quite recognised herself. It was true, she thought with a fresh burst of unease: Leo *did* see her through different eyes. But which was the real Ellie? The person she had known all her life, or this new person who only emerged when Leo Copeland was around?

It was a highly disturbing question, and one which she didn't want to answer. Not now, when Leo was so close and there were only the two of them in this silent, isolated tomb.

He levered himself away from the wall and took a step forward. Ellie's heart gave a sudden thump, and it sounded so loud that she was sure it must have echoed right round the enclosed chamber. What was he going to do now? She stiffened instinctively as her mind raced through all the possibilities.

To her surprise, though, he turned away from her, and headed towards the passage that led back towards the entrance.

'We're—we're leaving?' she croaked.

He turned back and shot a crooked smile at her. 'Do you want to stay?'

'Oh—no. No,' she repeated hurriedly. It was hard to be absolutely sure she was telling the truth, though, and she hoped Leo couldn't see any sign of her uncertainty and confusion on her face.

He was already walking off again, though, and Ellie stumbled thankfully along after him. What was it that happened to her whenever she was alone with Leo? she wondered a little dazedly. She seemed to be perfectly all right when other people were around, but once they were on their own she started thinking and behaving really strangely.

As soon as they stepped outside, the heat of the sun hit them like an almost physical blow, but she didn't even notice it. She was just hoping Leo wouldn't want to go into any more tombs. She was already trying to think of a good excuse to wait outside, if he did.

He seemed to have had enough of the Valley of the Kings, though. He turned and headed back towards the taxi, and Ellie gave a sigh of relief and trudged in the same direction.

They arrived back in Luxor late in the afternoon. Ellie went up to her room to change for dinner, and felt more comfortable once she was in her own clothes again. They might be rather dull, but at least she felt more like herself.

Leo was waiting for her in the dining-room. She was rather tense at first, wondering what he was going to say, but he kept the conversation light and undemanding all through dinner. Ellie finally began to relax and enjoy her meal. She could cope with him quite easily when he was like this. If only he would stay this way all the time!

When they had finished eating, he pushed his plate away and looked at her.

'I'm going to take some shots of the Nile. The sunsets around here are usually fairly spectacular and the river always looks best when it's catching the last light of day. More mysterious, more atmospheric. They're the kind of pictures that the producers of holiday brochures really go for.'

Ellie's dark brows drew together. 'Don't you ever stop working?'

'Of course,' Leo said at once. 'In fact, I don't mind leaving those pictures until tomorrow. What would you like to do instead?'

She wondered if she had imagined the husky note of invitation in his voice. Probably not! she decided.

And, in that case, she would feel a lot safer if his mind was fully occupied by work.

'No, that's all right,' she said hastily. 'Let's go ahead with the photos.'

As they left the hotel and walked towards the river, the sun was already sliding slowly towards the horizon. The sky was beginning to glow with shades of red, yellow and orange, and the buildings of Luxor caught and reflected the colours. And the Nile itself, when they finally reached it, had taken on a completely new character. The tall masts of the feluccas were silhouetted blackly against the vivid colours of the sky, and the water shimmered softly, looking as dark and mysterious as Leo had promised it would.

He took out his camera straight away, expertly focusing and making adjustments for the fading light before taking a rapid succession of pictures. Ellie watched with grudging admiration. When it came to photography, he certainly knew his stuff.

When the vivid shades of the sunset finally began to darken and fade, Leo put his camera away again and slung the case over his shoulder.

'That should do it,' he said with some satisfaction.

Ellie looked at him in some surprise. 'You're not going to take any more pictures?'

'No. The light's going now. Anyway, I've got all I need.'

'Then what am I doing here?' she demanded a little indignantly. 'If you didn't want me in any of the shots, I could have stayed back at the hotel.'

'I like having you with me,' he replied in an unruffled tone. 'I thought you knew that by now.'

'I don't know any such thing,' Ellie retorted. 'And I wish you'd stop saying things like that!'

'Why? Don't you like hearing them?'

'They just seem—unnecessary.'

Leo smiled gently. 'They seem fairly necessary to me.'

'You're weird,' she muttered. 'I should have guessed that when you turned up at the Pyramids dressed as an Egyptian guide!'

His gaze remained undisturbed. 'Do you think it's weird to want to spend more time with you?'

Ellie wasn't sure how to answer that, so she said nothing at all. Instead, she turned and stared at the river. The waters of the Nile stretched out in front of them, wide and tranquil, undisturbed now by the busy river traffic that churned up and down during the day.

She didn't feel tranquil, though. The calm beauty of the evening didn't seem to be having any effect on her at all.

What was affecting her was Leo. The last light from the dying sun glinted on his hair, giving it flame-bright highlights, and yet his eyes seemed more shadowed than usual, although a brief flare lit them as they locked on to her own darkening gaze.

She tried to remind herself that she had known him for only a very short time. He really wasn't as familiar as he suddenly seemed. And, when that didn't seem to be working, she told herself she ought to turn away from him and go straight back to the hotel. There was something about the gathering evening, the cool and yet somehow exotic atmosphere, that seemed to be having a really odd effect on her.

Leo drifted closer, scarcely appearing to move and yet somehow ending up only inches away.

Perhaps it was because he had moved so slowly and silently that he didn't actually alarm her. Now that she thought about it, she realised she couldn't remember him making any sudden moves in all the time she had known him.

He was like a great cat, she thought with a small shudder. Instinctively knowing that he mustn't frighten his prey.

And that was what she was, she now realised. His prey. She supposed she had suspected it from the very beginning, but this was the first time she had actually admitted it out loud.

Yet the thought didn't alarm her as much as it should have. It was almost *nice* to be stalked by someone like Leo Copeland. Dangerous, of course, but she had known that all along. And it hadn't stopped her from coming to Luxor with him.

Ellie tried to work out what all this signified, but finally decided she would rather not know. And all the time she was thinking it through Leo was standing there and silently watching her, as if waiting for her to reach some sort of conclusion.

Rather nervously, she cleared her throat. 'I—I suppose we should be getting back to the hotel.'

'Yes, I suppose we should,' he agreed. He didn't move, though. Nor did Ellie.

The sun had very nearly vanished now. Only a thin sliver remained above the horizon, and that would be gone in another few moments. The sky was still splashed with the colours of its fading rays, but darkness was rapidly creeping in, adding shadowed undertones. The intimacy of night was closing in on them, and Ellie could feel her own mood changing as the last of the light ebbed away.

She realised that, for the first time in ages, she didn't feel alone. And it was Leo who had somehow chased away the haunting sense of isolation. She didn't know how he had done it; she only knew that she liked it.

There was a new warmth inside her, and she wanted to cling on to it for as long as she could.

'Perhaps this *is* a good time to go back to the hotel,' Leo suggested softly.

Ellie didn't argue with him. She turned away from the river, every nerve in her body now aware of his presence as he fell into step beside her.

He made no effort to touch her, though. He didn't even hold her hand. Instead, they walked along in silence, perfectly in step, the last of the daylight now giving way to a black, starlit night.

Back at the hotel, they went directly up to the first floor. Ellie opened the door to her room and went inside. Without asking permission, Leo followed her in.

Her heart suddenly began to thump a little harder. This wasn't sensible, she told herself shakily. She ought to put a stop to it. And right now, before it all got completely out of hand.

So why didn't she?

Because she didn't want to, came the immediate reply. And Leo *knew* she didn't want to.

'Some things seem inevitable, right from the very beginning,' he said in a low tone, speaking out loud for the first time since they had left the river. 'Perhaps it's time to accept it, Ellie.'

'No,' she said, although without as much determination as she had intended.

'Why not?'

'Because——' Her voice came out in a dry rasp, and she quickly cleared her throat. 'Because I don't do things like this,' she answered more clearly.

A faint smile spread over his face. 'Everyone does things like this, Ellie,' he assured her huskily. 'But if you really don't want to, just tell me right now and I'll go away.'

She swallowed hard. She wanted to say just that, and yet the words wouldn't seem to come out. In the end, she gave a slow, helpless shake of her head. 'I don't want you to go,' she admitted, her voice little more than a reluctant whisper.

'Tell me why,' he pressed her gently.

'Because—because I don't want to be on my own,' she blurted out. An instant later she wished she hadn't said it. She hated admitting to the loneliness that still dogged her. Somehow, giving in to it, admitting it existed, always seemed to make it even worse.

Leo's gaze fixed on her. 'People who say something like that are usually people who are on their own far too much,' he observed quietly. 'Don't you have anyone who's close to you, Ellie?'

But she didn't want him to probe any deeper. 'I don't think that's any of your business,' she muttered.

'I think it is,' he replied. 'You see, I don't want to be just someone who fills in a few lonely hours.'

She blinked in sheer surprise. She hadn't been expecting him to say anything like that.

'What——?' Her voice came out croakily again, and she had to make another effort to clear her throat. 'What *do* you want to be, then?'

Leo's mouth curled into a slow smile. 'You want an honest answer? I'm not sure yet. I haven't quite worked it out. But I'm beginning to think this might be a good time to go into the whole thing a little more deeply.'

'What do you mean? How can we do that?'

'I thought we could start like this.'

His kiss was smooth as silk. Ellie hadn't been expecting it—not yet—and found herself yielding to it. If he had given her time, she might have had a chance to get her defences back into place. He had an unerring instinct for picking the right moment, though, and now he had caught her off balance he began to pursue his advantage single-mindedly. And she soon realised that he had no intention of letting her recover her senses.

That discovery came as quite a shock, because he had seemed outwardly so relaxed and undemanding. His second kiss, following so closely behind his first that she scarcely had time to draw breath, soon dispelled that illusion, though. Ellie began to discover that there were two Leos. The Leo who would refrain from even touching her because he didn't want to scare her off, and the other Leo who wanted her badly—*very* badly—and didn't seem prepared to wait any longer.

She remembered him telling her once that he was very good at this, and she was now finding out that he had told the truth. His hands moved with consummate skill, and his mouth seemed to trail fire as it moved from her lips to the soft, vulnerable skin at the base of her throat.

'I don't know what it is about you, Ellie Mitchell,' he murmured in a rather indistinct voice, 'but I just don't seem able to resist you.'

Ellie didn't dare admit—even to herself—that he had the power to make her feel exactly the same way. Anyway, there wasn't time. His mouth had restlessly returned to hers, subjecting her to a series of kisses that sent her senses reeling.

Was this love? she wondered in sudden giddy astonishment. She didn't know. She didn't have enough experience to judge. And, if it was, how had it happened? Why hadn't she seen it coming?

It couldn't be love, she decided shakily. It was far too soon. *Too soon.*

Yet how long did it take?

Leo's fingers tugged impatiently at the buttons on her blouse. He gave a grunt of satisfaction as he gained access to the warmth of her body underneath, and immediately edged closer. Ellie could smell the fresh muskiness of his hot skin; she could feel his forearms brushing against her as his hands worked their way round to her back, to unfasten the catch on her light cotton bra.

'Do you like this?' he murmured.

'Yes,' she whispered back, although she hadn't meant to.

'Do you like *me*?' When she didn't answer straight away, he kissed her a little more roughly. 'Do you, Ellie?'

She had the feeling that her reply was very important to him.

'Yes,' she muttered again, in an even lower voice.

Leo seemed to relax a fraction.

'How much?'

His persistent questioning was making her uneasy. Anyway, how could she answer him when she didn't even understand what was happening to her?

'Don't talk,' she said unsteadily, trying to distract him. 'Just touch me.'

'Hell,' he said with unexpected helplessness. 'How can I resist an invitation like that?'

His hands returned with new persuasiveness, followed by the warmth of his mouth as he bent his head to the softness of her breasts.

'You taste different from anyone else,' he murmured at last. 'But I suppose I should have expected that.'

Ellie stiffened briefly. She didn't want to think of all the other women who had shared these intimate caresses with Leo.

He felt her sudden tension, but didn't seem to realise what had caused it. Instead, he simply concentrated on soothing it away with a light, gentle stroking that melted her muscles into a state of pure relaxation.

She could feel the pressure of his body now, but he wasn't demanding anything from her yet. Instead, he was easing her towards the bed, taking her slowly but inexorably towards the next step.

Ellie blinked. Was she really going to let him do this? A couple of days ago—a couple of hours ago— her answer would have been a very definite no. Things had somehow changed since then, though, become confused, her emotions tossed into fast-growing chaos by the simple touch of his hands.

'I don't do this sort of thing,' she said shakily. Had she told him that before? She seemed to remember that she had.

This time Leo didn't even bother to answer her. He seemed to know that it had only been a very feeble protest, and one that he could easily override.

Ellie found herself lying on the bed, with Leo stretched out beside her. He seemed very relaxed again, and ready to take things at an easy pace. She wasn't so easily fooled this time, though. She knew what lay underneath that lazy façade.

As if to confirm it, she laid her hand lightly against his chest. His heart thumped rapidly against her palm, and she could feel the heat of his skin burning through the thin material of his shirt.

'Don't worry,' he murmured. 'It won't get out of control. Not yet.'

He leant over her and allowed his mouth to mark another trail of kisses across her breasts and stomach. Ellie shivered lightly as his lips touched her. It felt so right, to be with him here like this.

The room was in darkness, but the shutters were open and a faint light filtered in from the starlit night outside. Enough to see the expression on Leo's face as he drew back from her a fraction. Enough to see the outline of his body as he easily shrugged off his clothes.

Strong and powerful—Ellie had known he would look like that. She had already seen him stripped to the waist, when they had shared the compartment on the train. Now he was naked from head to foot, and not in the least embarrassed about it. Nor the fact that she could clearly see that he was already deeply aroused by her.

His hands eased away the last of her own clothes, and she made no effort to stop him. Her body felt totally languid, and incapable of any resistance.

'You're lovely,' he murmured, his gaze raking over her. 'But I knew you would be.'

'How could you possibly know something like that?' she whispered.

'I've no idea. I just seem very sure of certain things, where you're concerned.' His fingers drifted over her hips, settled on the flat plane of her stomach, making her muscles quiver. 'For instance, I know what you like. What will please you,' he said huskily.

His fingers suddenly dipped lower, and Ellie's eyes shot open with shock and pleasure.

'I wonder if you know what will please me?' he added invitingly.

And she did. She had no idea how she had come by such knowledge, but she knew instinctively what to do.

Her own hands reached out and began to touch, tentatively at first, and then with more confidence as he responded with small grunts of deep pleasure. Her fingertips registered warm skin, hard muscle, an inner quivering, and then a leaping response as her touch became even more bold.

'I can't keep up these games forever,' Leo warned thickly, suddenly drawing back from her. 'In fact, I think I'm pretty near my limit.'

Ellie didn't hear him. She was becoming lost in this new world of warmth and closeness and shared intimacy. She hadn't known it could be like this, and she desperately wanted to hold on to it for a while longer.

She laid her hands against him again, and loved the way he felt. Warm and vital and solid against her palms, powerful enough to force her into anything, if he wished, but gentle enough never to use that strength against her.

Leo responded to her touch with a faint groan of self-imposed frustration. Then, as if he had reached the point where he couldn't stop himself, he leant over her again, subjecting her to a series of caresses that were unexpectedly fierce.

Ellie didn't shrink away. Instead she found her body leaping to life under his touch, pressing eagerly against his hands as they moved over her breasts, opening up to him as they slid to the silky smoothness of her thighs.

His mouth returned to hers, telling her without words that he was fast approaching the point of no return. In an equally silent answer, her arms went round him and pulled his hard, demanding body even closer.

The shadows of the night gave way to a new kind of darkness as Leo moved over her. Ellie sank gladly down into the blackness, and found it was lined with velvet. A soft, silken-smooth pleasure that was utterly unlike anything she had ever known before.

Leo's movements became swifter, and the pleasure increased, coming in waves now, each one seemingly designed to drown her in the most exquisite way possible. She could hear the sound of strangled breathing, and didn't know if it was coming from her or Leo— or perhaps both of them.

Then her body seemed to tense and stand still for a split instant. Leo must have sensed it, because he raised his head, locked his brilliant gaze on to hers and dragged in a long, shuddering breath.

'Now, Ellie,' he muttered, his voice turning her name into a molten caress. *'Now!'*

One final, fierce thrust of his body accompanied that last word. The hot, delicious friction triggered an instant response, and the last wave of all began to roll over her. Ellie heard the breath catch haltingly in her throat. Then she surrendered willingly to its force as it swept and tossed them both into a sea of mindless, endless delight.

CHAPTER EIGHT

ELLIE woke up the next morning to a sense of warmth and happiness that was quite foreign to her. For a few moments she couldn't understand it. Then her mind locked on to one word. *Leo*——

She turned her head and found that the bed beside her was empty. The sheets still felt warm, though. He must have left only minutes ago.

She was almost glad he wasn't here. It gave her a chance to think about last night. To try and work out what had happened.

But you know what happened, a wry voice inside her head reminded her. Leo made love to you. And you didn't just let him—you *wanted* him to.

Yet why had she wanted him to? Ellie wasn't sure she was ready to answer that question right now. The reply was already being given by that annoyingly persistent voice inside her head, though.

Because you're falling in love with the man. It's been happening slowly but surely over the last couple of days, and the only reason you haven't realised it before is that you've been stubbornly determined to ignore all these new feelings he's aroused in you.

But he's a stranger, she argued a little desperately with herself.

Yet that argument just didn't hold up. She didn't feel as if Leo had *ever* been a stranger. Perhaps that was one of the most disturbing things about him, this sense of familiarity that he evoked.

Just at that moment, the door opened and Leo walked in. Ellie gulped. She really wasn't ready to face him yet.

He was fully dressed, and looked bright and alert. He didn't come right into the room, though, but stopped just a couple of feet inside the doorway.

'It isn't that I don't want to come near you,' he told her. 'Quite the opposite, in fact,' he added, with a grin. 'But this is a Muslim country, and they have very fixed ideas about what's permissible between an unmarried man and a woman. I don't want to shock the hotel staff by letting them find me in your room first thing in the morning.' When she didn't answer, he looked at her a little quizzically. 'Isn't there anything you want to say to me?' he prompted.

Ellie couldn't get out a single word, though. The sight of him standing there, tawny gold hair gleaming, his eyes glittering a little wickedly, seemed to have struck her totally dumb.

'I don't usually have this effect on women,' Leo said drily. 'Most of them say too much the morning after! But there are quite a few things that I think we do have to talk about. Have a shower and get dressed, and I'll see you down in the dining-room.'

She had the feeling that he was reluctant to leave the room, but he did eventually turn around and walk out, closing the door firmly behind him.

Ellie let out a great sigh of pent-up breath. She wasn't sure her nerves were up to this! She could hardly stay in bed all day, though, so she hauled her languid body into the bathroom and stood under a cool shower until she began to feel a little more like herself.

After she had dressed, she dusted just a light coating of make-up on to her face. There wasn't much point in slapping more on, to try and give herself confidence. No amount of make-up could disguise her huge, over-bright eyes or the flush of colour on her cheeks.

At last she couldn't put it off any longer. Slowly, and on legs that were infuriatingly unsteady, she made her way down to the dining-room.

As he had promised, Leo was waiting for her. Breakfast was spread out in front of him, but he didn't look as if he had touched any of it.

Ellie slid into her seat and kept her eyes carefully lowered.

'First you won't talk to me,' he commented with some amusement. 'Now you won't even look at me. We're not going to get very far like this, Ellie.'

She remembered the last time he had spoken her name—and her response!—and blushed furiously.

'I didn't realise until now that you were such a shy girl,' he said, not sounding at all displeased by his discovery.

'There's an awful lot you don't know about me,' she mumbled.

'I know,' he agreed. 'But there's plenty of time to do something about that.' He pushed a plate towards her. 'You'd better try and eat something. I've a heavy schedule mapped out for this morning, and I don't want you collapsing on me from lack of food.'

That finally made her head snap up. 'You're going to work?' she said disbelievingly. 'This morning?'

'Unromantic, isn't it?' he agreed. 'But I've got to be back in London by the end of the week. That leaves me just four days to finish this assignment, and I've still got to fit in a visit to Aswan and the temple of Abu Simbel.'

Hearing him talk about his return to London brought Ellie sharply back to reality. He had a whole life there that she knew absolutely nothing about. She didn't even know if he intended to try and fit her into it.

'I suppose your family must be missing you by now,' she said slowly. 'Or are they used to you being away for long stretches at a time?'

'I don't live at home,' he told her. 'I haven't done since I was eighteen. That doesn't stop my mother fussing over me, of course. And she sends my sisters along at regular intervals to check that I'm eating properly and wearing clean underwear.' He gave a shrug of wry resignation. 'I suppose parents are always loath to admit that their children have finally grown up.' He poured some coffee and handed her a cup. 'Do yours still fuss over you?'

The old lies hovered on the tip of Ellie's tongue. Then she firmly pushed them to one side. If she couldn't tell the truth to Leo, whom could she tell it to?

'My parents are dead,' she said in a clear and steady voice. 'They died when I was quite young.'

Leo's expression changed. 'But you told me your father was retired.'

'I know,' she said in a low tone. 'I lied to you. I lie about it to everyone. I never tell people the truth. They always start to look so sorry for me, and I hate that.'

He was silent for quite some time. 'If they died when you were young, who brought you up?' he asked at last.

'My grandparents. They were very good to me— gave me lots of love, and spoilt me when I needed it.'

He was looking at her intently now. '*Were* good to you?' he queried, his tawny eyes darkening. 'They're dead as well?'

Ellie nodded, because suddenly she didn't quite trust herself to say anything.

'What about brothers and sisters?'

'I had a sister,' she said at length, in a low voice. 'She died at the same time as my parents. There was a fire——'

'You've no one?' he said a little disbelievingly. 'Not even aunts or uncles? *No one?*'

She somehow managed a feeble smile. 'The original orphan. Except that you can't be an orphan at my age, can you? It just sounds silly.'

Leo was hardly listening to her, though. Instead, he slowly shook his head. 'I've always been surrounded by family. I can't imagine what it would be like to be without them.'

'It's lonely,' said Ellie in a small, tight voice. 'Very lonely.'

He poured himself a cup of coffee, as if he needed to give himself time to think.

'I don't know quite what to say to you,' he said at last.

'There's nothing you *can* say,' she replied in a much steadier tone. 'And it's all right, really. I've got used to it. I can live with it. I certainly don't want you to feel sorry for me,' she warned.

'That isn't the way I feel about you at all,' he said slowly. 'But it might change one or two things——'

As his voice broke off and a dark frown furrowed his forehead, Ellie looked at him uneasily.

'What sort of things?'

He made an obvious effort to relax, as if he realised that she had faced enough emotional turmoil over the last few hours.

'For a start, this isn't the sort of conversation I'd intended having with you this morning,' he said wryly. 'But the things I *was* going to say to you suddenly don't seem very appropriate.' He pushed his undrunk coffee to one side, and seemed to reach a decision. 'Look,' he said in a firmer voice, 'let's take a breather for a while. I'll forget about work, you forget about— well, anything you *want* to forget about. We'll just walk around Luxor, relax, and steer completely clear of personal subjects for a couple of hours.'

'What about your schedule?' asked Ellie.

'To hell with the schedule. Some things are more important than photographs.' His mouth became less set and he almost smiled. 'Not many things—but I think you count as one of them.'

She began to feel much happier again. A couple of hours of Leo's company, with undemanding conversation and no great emotional decisions to be faced, were just what she needed right now.

They left the hotel and began to walk along amicably side by side, not touching, but with very little distance between them. The sun was blazing down brightly, but it wasn't scorchingly hot yet.

'Where do you want to go?' asked Leo. 'Down to the river?'

'No, not the river,' said Ellie, rather quickly. Although its spell wouldn't be as strong in daylight as it was around the bewitching time of sunset, she still thought it would be better to avoid it for a while. 'Let's look round the shops,' she suggested.

He gave a faint groan, but gave in gracefully. And he quite seemed to enjoy himself as they wandered in and out of shops and poked around market stalls, some piled high with tourist junk, while others offered genuine bargains and a good quality of craftsmanship.

By late morning, Ellie finally began to wilt. Leo immediately noticed, and steered her towards a nearby restaurant.

'Let's have an early lunch,' he suggested.

She was surprised to find she was starving. She ordered chicken, with side dishes of rice and vegetables, and then was amazed when she heard Leo ordering spaghetti.

'Spaghetti?' she echoed in disbelief. 'You're going to eat spaghetti in *Egypt*?'

'I like it,' he said in an untroubled tone.

'You'll get fat,' she warned, when she saw the heaped dish that the waiter set in front of him.

'I never put on weight,' Leo said comfortably. 'Stick around until I'm an old man, and you'll know I'm telling the truth.'

That last remark definitely distracted Ellie from her chicken. 'Stick around until I'm an old man', he had said. Was that an invitation? If it was, it was a very oblique one, and he hadn't said anything further to clarify it.

Better forget about it for now, she warned herself silently. Don't push things when the morning's going so well. Remember Steven. You pushed *him*—and you lost him. Don't make the same stupid mistake again, because this time it's so much more important.

She tried to concentrate on her food, and finally managed to clear her plate. Leo still hadn't said anything more, although she glanced up a couple of times and caught him looking at her in a rather odd way. She had the impression that he was rather more tense than he had been earlier, and not really tasting the food he was eating.

They finished the meal with coffee, although Leo barely touched his. Then he pushed the cup away and leant forward.

'Ellie, this isn't a good time or place, but I think I need to say this right now,' he said rather rapidly. 'I want——'

'Leo?' An unfamiliar male voice boomed out from behind them, making Ellie jump slightly. 'Leo, it *is* you. I knew I recognised the back of that head!'

Ellie slowly turned round and found herself looking at a tall, blond-haired man in his early thirties, the same age as Leo.

A look of resignation crossed Leo's face. 'Hello, Philip,' he said, and Ellie had the feeling that he was forcing himself to be polite.

The newcomer drew up a chair and sat down. 'I didn't expect to bump into you in the middle of Egypt. What on earth are you doing here?'

'Taking photographs,' replied Leo briefly.

Philip turned to Ellie and grinned. 'Wherever Leo is, there's always a camera! I'm Philip Danby, by the way. Lawyer, respectable married man—although my wife's rather conveniently back in England at the moment—and long-time friend of Leo Copeland, the only bachelor left in our group.' His smile broadened. 'It doesn't look as if he's going to introduce you, so perhaps you'd better do it yourself.'

'I'm Ellie Mitchell,' Ellie said a little shyly. 'I'm——' She hesitated there, because she didn't know quite how to explain what she was doing here with Leo.

'Ellie's working for me,' Leo cut in. 'I'm featuring her in a series of photos that I'm doing.'

Since he didn't seem to want Philip to know that their relationship had begun to turn into something a lot more personal, Ellie didn't try to add anything to what he had said. In fact, she preferred it to remain a secret for a while. She felt as if she needed time to get used to it herself before anyone else was told.

'Look, why don't the two of you have dinner with me tonight?' invited Philip. 'I'm here for a couple of days with a colleague—a *male* colleague,' he added with a grin, as Leo looked at him quizzically. 'We're in Luxor on behalf of a client of ours, who has business connections in this part of the world. We're drawing up contracts, going over the fine print of agreements—you know the sort of thing. It's fairly standard stuff, though, so it leaves me with quite a lot of free time. I can easily fit in dinner. Or even lunch tomorrow, if that would suit you better.'

'We won't be here by lunchtime tomorrow,' Leo replied. 'We're moving on to Aswan in the morning. And I'm afraid we can't manage dinner this evening. I've too much work to fit in before we leave.'

His voice was regretful, but firm, and Ellie was left with the impression that he didn't actually want to have dinner with Philip.

'You're a workaholic,' Philip complained. 'But I've told you that before.'

'Yes, you have,' Leo agreed amicably. 'Look, we'll have lunch together when we're both back in London. Give me a ring, and we'll fix up a date.' He glanced at his watch and got to his feet. 'Sorry, but we've got to be going.' He gave Ellie a gentle tug on her elbow, and she got the message and also stood up.

'Goodbye,' she said with a rather apologetic smile, and let Leo hustle her out of the restaurant.

As soon as they got outside, she looked at him curiously. 'Didn't you want to have dinner with him?' she asked.

'Philip's an old friend, but he always wants to know what's going on in everyone's lives,' Leo replied briefly. 'I didn't want to face a barrage of personal questions—not yet. There's too much that we still haven't sorted out. Too many questions that *we* haven't answered.'

Ellie looked at him a little uncertainly. 'Do you want to talk about it?'

'Not right now. I'm not in the mood for talking. I'm going out with my camera for a couple of hours this afternoon. I want to get some shots of the temples of Karnak.'

Did he want her to go with him? she wondered uneasily. He hadn't actually said so, and she was suddenly nervous about asking him. He seemed to have withdrawn from her, almost as if he wanted to put some distance between them.

'I thought——' she began hesitantly. Then, in a steadier voice, she went on, 'I thought I might do some more shopping this afternoon. There are a couple of things I want to buy. That is, if you don't need me.'

She silently prayed for him to say that he *did* need her. That, even if he didn't want her to be in the photographs he planned to take, he still wanted her with him.

Leo immediately shook his head, though. 'Go shopping, if you want to. It's fine with me. We'll get together again this evening, for dinner.'

They had reached their hotel by this time, and Ellie began to turn towards the stairs, her feet suddenly feeling very heavy. Leo caught hold of her arm, though, and spun her back to face him.

'Don't read anything into this that isn't there,' he said softly. 'I just think it might be a good thing if we have a couple of hours away from each other.'

Ellie felt as if she didn't want to spend any time away from him, not ever, but this didn't seem like a good moment to tell him that. Instead, she nodded rather numbly, somehow managed a smile, then went slowly up to her room.

She stood at the window and watched as Leo left the hotel, his camera case slung over his shoulder. It was so easy to pick him out from the crowds of people that now thronged along the street below. Taller than most men, his tawny gold hair glinting in the sunlight, he drew her gaze like a magnet.

She watched him until he had completely disappeared from sight. Then she gave a small sigh and turned away.

What had been going through his head since he had left her bed this morning? She had no idea. She didn't even know where they were going from here—if anywhere. Leo had been oddly evasive about just about everything. Ellie hated this uncertainty, but at the same time she didn't dare ask any direct questions. Give him time, if that's what he needs, she told herself as she walked restlessly round the room.

But what if he took that time to decide that last night had been fine, but a one-off? That he didn't want to take it any further, or get more deeply involved?

Ellie gave a small shiver. She had been coping with her life so much better recently, but she didn't know if she could cope with that. Her mind shied painfully away from just the thought of it.

It hasn't happened yet, she reminded herself fiercely. Forget about it for a while. You told Leo you were going shopping. Well, go! Do something—*any-thing*—to take your mind off Leo Copeland.

She gathered up her bag and marched purposefully out of the hotel. It was very hot now, and the sun was blazing down with dazzling brightness, but she didn't even notice. Instead she headed straight for the souvenir shops, determined to browse around for an hour or two, letting the colourful items they had for sale distract her.

She was just sorting through some fairly inexpensive but pretty necklaces when she heard someone say her name. The voice sounded familiar, and she turned round to find herself facing Philip Danby.

'Souvenir-hunting?' he asked cheerfully. 'I'm doing the same thing. I'm trying to find something to take home for my wife.' He held up an exquisitely delicate gold chain. 'Do you think she'd like this?'

'I don't know your wife, so it's hard to say,' Ellie replied. 'But, if it's any help, *I'd* certainly love it.'

'Then I'll take it,' Philip said promptly. 'You look like a girl with good taste.'

He haggled over the price of the chain for a few minutes, and seemed satisfied with the amount of money he finally handed over. He tucked the chain into his pocket, then turned back to Ellie.

'This heat's a killer. Do you fancy a cold drink?'

Ellie was about to refuse, but then changed her mind. Suddenly she was quite eager to spend some time with this friend of Leo's. It might be a good chance to find out more about this enigmatic man who had barged into her life.

At a nearby restaurant, Philip ordered a cold beer for himself and fresh fruit juice for Ellie. Then he sat back and looked at her.

'Leo certainly knows how to pick girls,' he said admiringly. Then, as she stiffened a little, he went on quickly, 'Don't take that the wrong way. I only meant that he always manages to get really fantastic girls to pose for his photographs. Of course, it helps that he always knows exactly what kind of girl he wants. And, once he spots her, he'll move heaven and earth to get her!' He shot a grin at her. 'I've known him walk up to a complete stranger in the street, then stick to that girl like glue until she agrees to pose for him. Of course, she always does,' he added with a resigned shrug. 'Leo's so good with women. He's been like that ever since I first met him, at university. I used to watch him, to try and work out how he did it, but I never did figure it out. I think it was just something he was born with.'

Ellie sipped her juice, and remained uneasily silent. After all, what could she say? That that was the way Leo had approached *her*? That he had followed her all round Cairo, and not left her alone until he had got exactly what he wanted? It might be the truth, but there was no way she was going to admit that to this virtual stranger!

'Where did you meet Leo?' Philip asked casually.

'In Cairo,' she replied, after a short pause. 'I was— I was out of work, and he offered me this job. He wanted a model for the series of photographs he was doing, and I agreed to work for him since it meant earning some extra money.'

And that wasn't exactly a lie, she thought a little guiltily. Not quite the truth either, but that was only because she had left so much out.

'Then you and Leo have got a strictly working relationship?' asked Philip. A moment later, though, he shook his head. 'Sorry, I shouldn't have asked that. It's none of my business.'

'That's all right,' Ellie said rather stiffly. 'And yes, we have got a working relationship.'

That was something else that only bordered on the truth. Yet they *did* have a working relationship. It was just that they might now have something else as well—although Leo hadn't actually said as much, not yet.

'Try and make sure you keep it that way,' Philip advised, to her surprise.

Ellie looked up at him sharply. 'Why?' she asked, and hoped he couldn't hear the tense note in her voice.

'Leo's a heartbreaker,' he told her. 'He's been like that ever since I've known him. I don't even think it's entirely his fault. Women take one look at him and just fall over at his feet.' He grinned. 'I wish I had that knack! I'd have had a much more interesting life.' Then his face became more serious again. 'Remember what I've said, though. You seem like a nice girl, Ellie. Don't fall for Leo. Pose for his photos, take his money, then run.'

'Don't worry,' Ellie somehow managed to get out. 'I'm very good at keeping my feet firmly on the ground.'

'I'm sure you are,' agreed Philip. 'You look like a girl who's got a lot of common sense.' Then he gave a rather apologetic shrug. 'This conversation seems to keep getting rather personal. Sorry about that. It's just that you're very easy to talk to. I keep forgetting that we only met this morning.'

'That's all right,' said Ellie, with a rather forced smile. It wasn't, though, and she was beginning to wish she had turned down Philip Danby's invitation.

She was beginning to find out more about Leo than she wanted to know.

'How are the photo sessions going?' asked Philip, making an obvious effort to switch to a safer topic of conversation.

'Fairly well, I think,' replied Ellie, relieved at the change of subject. 'Leo seems to know exactly the kind of pictures that he wants.'

'He's good, isn't he?' agreed Philip. 'He could easily have been a professional photographer. Not as much money as his own line of work, of course, but probably the same kind of job satisfaction.'

His words made Ellie freeze up inside. She stared at him in numb astonishment for a few moments. Then she somehow managed to speak. 'He—he isn't a professional?' she got out in a tight voice.

Philip looked at her in surprise. 'You didn't know that?'

Rather desperately, she tried to recover herself. 'I—I just assumed that he was——'

'He's certainly as good as a professional,' said Philip. 'But photography's just a hobby, as far as Leo's concerned. Although a pretty absorbing hobby.'

'Then—what line of work *is* he in?' Ellie asked tautly.

'Computer software. He owns his own company— has done for several years now. He writes rather specialised and complicated computer programs, all hi-tech stuff—I don't really understand it,' Philip said cheerfully. 'I prefer to leave all that sort of thing to the experts.'

'And Leo's an expert?'

'You bet he is!'

And an expert in more fields than one, Ellie thought with some bitterness, realising how many lies Leo must have told her. An expert in getting his own way—in getting what he wanted. And probably in discarding it, when he had finished with it!

Abruptly, she stood up. 'I've—I've got to go.'

'So soon?' said Philip. 'Wouldn't you like another drink?'

She jerkily shook her head, and fumbled for her bag.

'Well, give my regards to Leo,' said Philip, not seeming to notice that anything was wrong. 'I'm sorry the two of you can't make it for dinner tonight.'

Ellie somehow choked out a goodbye, then hurried out of the restaurant.

She didn't remember anything about the walk back to the hotel. She wasn't aware of anything until she was back in her own room, with the door shut behind her. Then she slowly went over to stand by the window.

Philip's words kept echoing round and round inside her head. 'I've known him walk up to a complete stranger in the street, then stick to that girl like glue until she agrees to pose for him.' Well, that certainly sounded pretty familiar! 'Leo's so good with women.' Ellie remembered that he had told her that himself. The only trouble was, she hadn't realised then just *how* good he was. Leo wasn't a professional photographer. But he *was* a liar.

And, last of all—'Leo's a heartbreaker.' Ellie had the awful feeling that she was going to find that out for herself.

She was staring out of the window now, and she finally saw what she had been looking for. A tawny gold head that stood out from all the others around it.

Leo had the room next to hers, and a couple of minutes later she heard his door open, then close again. A flat expression entered her eyes, and her shoulders became visibly stiff. Then she left her own room and walked into his, without bothering to knock.

He turned round as she came in, and looked faintly surprised to see her.

'I thought you'd still be out shopping. Most women spend hours in the shops, once they get there.'

'And you know a lot about what "most women" like to do?' Ellie enquired coolly.

The faint smile that had touched his mouth disappeared. 'I didn't actually say that.'

'No, you didn't,' she agreed. 'But I dare say it's true. After all, you know such a lot about so many things.' She walked a little further into the room. 'Cameras, for instance,' she went on, her fingers trailing over the bag that held his photographic equipment. 'Lighting, exposure times, film speeds— but, of course, professional photographers are meant to know about those things, aren't they?'

Leo's eyes narrowed. 'What is this about, Ellie?'

'About?' she echoed thoughtfully. 'I suppose it's about getting to know you better. I've never felt that I really know you very well, which is funny when you come to think about it. Especially after last night.'

She somehow managed to keep her tone quite expressionless, although it cost her a great deal.

Leo prowled slowly around the room, his gaze never leaving her. 'Last night was good,' he said at last.

'Yes, it was,' she agreed, amazed at the way she was managing to keep so controlled. 'But you probably knew it would be. You'd already told me how good you were at it, and you certainly weren't lying about *that*!'

His brows drew together in the beginnings of a dark frown. 'Are you trying to say that I lied about something else?'

She gave a small shrug. 'I didn't actually say that.' She touched his camera bag again. 'I think I'd like to know more about your work,' she said, lifting her head and looking directly at him. 'In particular, I'd like to know more about this assignment of yours. Photos for a holiday brochure—that's what you said, isn't it?'

'You know damned well that's what I said,' he growled. 'Where's this leading, Ellie?'

'Who knows? Perhaps we'll even eventually get to the truth. How about telling me how you got this assignment?'

'The man who runs the holiday agency is a friend of mine. He asked me to take the photos.'

'And exactly how much is he paying you?' Ellie asked him, her voice still remarkably calm.

Leo's tawny eyes suddenly glowed. 'You know, don't you?' he said abruptly.

And then, without any warning, the venom suddenly poured out of her.

'Yes, I know,' she hissed back at him. 'I know you're a liar! I know you're not a professional photographer! I know you like to pick up girls in the street and persuade them to model for you. And I bet they all end up in the same place. In your bed! You're right, Leo. I know!'

He glared at her fiercely. 'You're making it sound planned, and you're making it sound sordid!'

'Oh, I am sorry about that,' she responded with cutting sarcasm. 'But, before we start to argue about whether you planned the whole thing, or just picked me up on an impulse, I'd like to get a few more things straight. Let's start with your long list of expenses. Professional photographers get expenses. Amateurs don't. So who paid for everything, Leo? The train trip from Cairo, the hotel bills, the clothes and the meals, and all the other little extras?'

He looked as if he dearly didn't want to answer. He flashed a black look at her, but Ellie refused to wilt. Instead, she stared straight back at him and, amazingly, he was the one to look away.

'I did,' he muttered at last.

'You did,' she repeated, and this time her tone was quite flat. 'Every penny came out of your own pocket. You bought me, then paid for me every step of the way. Do you know what that makes me feel like, Leo?'

'I intended to tell you,' he growled.

'Of course you did. But the question is, when? After we'd made love again tonight? After we'd moved on to Aswan, and slept our way through some of Egypt's most luxurious hotels?' Ellie's eyes abruptly hardened. 'And, since you're so free with your money, were you going to pay me for sleeping with you as well?'

Leo swung round with sudden ferociousness and looked as if he wanted to hit her. Ellie didn't see him, though. She was already running through the doorway, her eyes hopelessly blurred with tears.

CHAPTER NINE

BACK in her room, Ellie immediately began to pack. Every single one of her nerves was acutely on edge, waiting for Leo to come charging through the door, his temper blazing. It didn't happen, though. She finished packing her bags and left the room without even seeing him.

The tears were gone from her eyes now. Instead, they seemed to have settled somewhere inside her chest in a hard, painful lump that wouldn't budge. She decided to ignore it. It couldn't stay there forever; it would have to go away at *some* time.

She walked over to the reception desk and asked for her bill.

'You're leaving?' asked the clerk in surprise. 'But you're booked in until tomorrow.'

'I've changed my plans,' Ellie told him in a toneless voice.

He checked through some papers, then smiled at her. 'There is nothing to pay. Everything is to be put on Mr Copeland's account.'

'I wish to pay my own bill,' she replied at once. 'Please work out what I owe you.'

The clerk looked at her as if she were mad. Then he gave a small sigh, and began to make some calculations.

Ellie handed over the sum he eventually asked for, picked up her case, and left the hotel. She decided to walk to the station. It would save money, and that was going to be in fairly short supply from now on.

She eventually managed to find out that there was a train leaving for Cairo at seven-thirty that evening, arriving early the next morning. On impulse, she handed over enough money to pay for a sleeping compartment. She suddenly couldn't stand the thought of spending the long journey in the company of strangers.

You're mad, she told herself with a shake of her head. You walk to the station to save the taxi fare, then spend all that money on a sleeper! It was too late to change her mind now, though. Instead she went to wait for the train, all the time glancing nervously over her shoulder because part of her couldn't quite believe that Leo would let her go so easily.

Face it, she lectured herself wearily—the whole thing was a set-up from beginning to end. It was just a game to him, picking you up like that, buying you clothes, pretending to take all those photos, paying for first-class travel and luxury hotels. All the time, he was just a hunter cleverly stalking his prey. And you fell for it! You've been incredibly stupid and naïve, Ellie Mitchell.

Although she had the small sleeper compartment to herself, she stayed wide awake all through the endlessly long night. It was so hard to accept that she was back to square one, jobless and alone, when just hours ago it had seemed that her life was actually going to change for the better for once.

She thought about all the promises Leo had made to her, and her face became hostile. He had said she would earn good money from this assignment, but he hadn't told her that every single penny of it would come from him—*if* he had even intended to give it to her. He might have just disappeared once they reached Aswan, saving himself that extra expense. And then there had been his promise to introduce her to a reputable modelling agency. Ha! snorted Ellie disbelievingly. She must have been really feeble-minded to have fallen for that one!

Then the brief spurt of hostility drained away again, and the deep misery crept back. And, since there didn't seem any way of getting rid of it, she curled up into a small ball and hoped this awful night would soon come to an end.

The train rattled into Cairo early in the morning. Tired and depressed, Ellie gathered up her case, got off the train and slowly trudged out of the station.

She realised she had no idea where to go. All she had been able to think about yesterday was getting away from Luxor—and from Leo.

She forced her tired brain to face this new problem, and could only come up with one solution. She still had her original air ticket back to England, but the flight wasn't due to leave until tomorrow. That meant she would have to spend tonight in a hotel. And she supposed it might as well be the hotel she had stayed in before. At least it would save her the added hassle of trying to find somewhere else.

She took a taxi to the hotel. More expense! she warned herself grimly, but she was just too tired to walk.

The hotel clerk looked surprised to see her back, but soon found her a room. Ellie took the key, told him she could manage her own luggage, and plodded up the stairs.

Once inside the room, she dumped her case in the corner and left it, then collapsed on to the bed, still fully clothed. After her sleepless night and the trauma of the last few hours, physical exhaustion was sweeping over her. Ellie closed her eyes and, only seconds later, fell into a restless sleep.

When she opened her eyes again, she found it was almost lunchtime. She sat up slowly, then gave a faint groan as the memories began flooding back. There was so much still to be faced, and right now she just didn't feel up to it.

You'll feel better after a shower and a meal, she tried to persuade herself.

The shower did freshen her up, but she wasn't at all sure she could face any food yet. She realised she hadn't eaten for twenty-four hours, though, and knew it would be stupid to starve herself. She would only end up feeling far worse than she did already.

She reluctantly went down to the dining-room, and sat by herself at a small table in the corner. The waiter brought her some soup, and she was just trying to force down a few mouthfuls when a familiar voice drifted through the doorway.

'Come along, girls,' instructed Miss Mason's brisk tones. 'We've just time for a quick lunch before one final visit to the Egyptian Museum.'

Ellie blinked. Miss Mason and the group of girls? Back here in Cairo?

Then she remembered that they had been scheduled to return to Cairo on the last day of the trip, ready to fly back to England the following morning. Ellie briefly closed her eyes. How could she possibly have forgotten that? If she had remembered, she would certainly have booked herself into another hotel. She

didn't want to see *anyone* she knew right now, and
that definitely included Miss Mason and the rest of
the school party!

She hurriedly lowered her head and hoped they
wouldn't see her. It was already too late, though. She
could hear a couple of the girls muttering her name,
and looked up to find Miss Mason was staring at her
with some disapproval.

She somehow managed a feeble smile and concentrated on her soup again, only to find it was proving
incredibly difficult to swallow. She choked down a
couple more mouthfuls, then just nibbled at the salad
that followed.

To her relief, Miss Mason and the girls ate quickly,
then filed out of the dining-room. Several of the girls
had shot curious glances and then shy smiles at her,
and Ellie had forced herself to smile back. Since the
tickets for the school party had been booked as a
block, she would be flying back on the same plane as
them tomorrow, so she might as well make the best
of it.

She had absolutely no inclination to go sightseeing
in Cairo, so she spent the rest of the afternoon in the
hotel lounge. She still felt tired, miserable, and horribly edgy. The future loomed in front of her, empty
and uncertain, and she didn't know yet what she was
going to do about it.

Then, late in the afternoon, one possible solution
popped into her head. Why not try to get her old job
back?

Because Miss Mason won't give it to you, she
answered herself at once. It's useless even to try.

But there was a part of Ellie that didn't want anything to do with the old feelings of pessimism any

more. All right, so the answer would almost certainly be no. But it wouldn't hurt at least to have a go.

She waited rather tensely for Miss Mason's return. Then, at five o'clock, she heard the group of girls clattering back into the hotel, closely followed by Miss Mason, who instructed them to go directly up to their rooms and get ready for the evening meal.

Before Miss Mason could follow them up the stairs, Ellie walked over to her.

'Could I talk to you for a few minutes?' she asked directly.

Miss Mason didn't look at all pleased by her request. 'I really think I've already said everything that needed to be said to you, Miss Mitchell.'

'I'm only asking for a very small amount of your time,' Ellie replied, slightly amazed that her voice was coming out so steadily and politely.

'Well—all right,' agreed Miss Mason, with obvious reluctance. She followed Ellie back into the lounge, seated herself opposite her, back very upright and ankles neatly crossed, and looked directly at her.

'Well, what is it you want?' she enquired. 'A reference? That might be rather difficult, under the circumstances.'

'No, I don't want a reference,' Ellie answered. 'I'm asking you for another chance. I'd like my job back.'

Miss Mason looked absolutely astonished that she had even had the nerve to ask. Before she had the chance to refuse outright, though, Ellie quickly began talking again.

'I know you fired me because you thought I was setting the girls a low moral standard, but things weren't at all the way they seemed. The man you saw me with—he wasn't in my room because I invited him there. He more or less forced his way in. He kept pestering me, you see. I couldn't get rid of him.'

And that was very near to the truth—at least at the beginning.

'I certainly didn't spend the whole of that afternoon in my room with him,' Ellie went on. 'I walked out and left him there, because that was the only way I could get away from him. I came down here, to the hotel lounge, and I stayed here for the rest of the afternoon. Ask the hotel staff—they'll confirm that I'm telling the truth. Some of them must have seen me in here.'

For a moment Miss Mason looked as if she almost believed Ellie's story. Then she firmly shook her head again.

'When we went back to your room, to collect the guidebook, that man came out of your bathroom,' she reminded Ellie, her voice laced with deep disapproval.

'But I didn't know he was there! And I certainly didn't give him permission to use my shower. Look,' Ellie went on urgently, 'if I'd known he was there, would I have let you walk in and find him? I knew perfectly well how you felt about such things. If I'd really spent the afternoon with that man, I'd have done everything I could to prevent you finding out about it. I wouldn't have let you anywhere near that room until I was absolutely sure he'd gone.'

Miss Mason's severe brows drew together thoughtfully. 'I'm willing to admit you do have a point there,' she said at last. 'But you still haven't adequately explained how you got involved with this man in the first place. I find it hard to believe he just appeared out of the blue and began following you around.'

'But that's exactly what *did* happen.' Vivid memories suddenly flashed into Ellie's mind, and she saw Leo standing in the doorway of that room in the Egyptian Museum; Leo following her around the bazaar; Leo dressed up as an Egyptian guide at the Pyramids. She briefly closed her eyes and nearly faltered. Then she took a deep, steadying breath and reminded herself how much she needed this job. She somehow had to convince Miss Mason that she was suitable for re-employment.

'He really just wouldn't leave me alone,' she went on quickly. 'There wasn't anything I could do about it.'

'But you've managed to get rid of him now?' Miss Mason questioned her. 'Can you give me a firm assurance that there won't be any repeat of those incidents?'

'Yes, he's gone,' Ellie confirmed quietly. That, at least, was the truth. Leo Copeland wouldn't be back, not after those things she had said to him.

Miss Mason was silent for a long time, and Ellie waited edgily for her decision. It would make all the difference to her if she could get this job back. She would have something to cling on to, to help get her through the bad patch she knew lay ahead.

'I believe it's only fair to give you the benefit of the doubt,' Miss Mason said crisply at last. 'I understand that girls do sometimes attract unwanted attention from men, and I'm willing to accept that you got yourself into a situation that you simply didn't know how to handle.'

And that was something of an understatement! Ellie thought grimly. But it looked as if something was finally going to go right for her.

'Then I can have my job back?' she asked, wanting to hear Miss Mason actually say it.

'I'm willing to re-employ you—although strictly on a trial basis,' Miss Mason warned her. 'You may join us for the evening meal, and I expect you to help supervise our departure from Cairo tomorrow morning.'

Ellie knew she should feel guilty because there was so much she *hadn't* told Miss Mason. She also knew she should feel pleased and relieved that she had got her job back. She didn't seem capable of feeling anything very much at all at the moment, though. Instead, she said a rather stiff 'thank you'. Then she escaped up to her room, where she sat on the edge of the bed and numbly wondered how she was going to face the next few days.

She got through the evening meal by concentrating hard on the food and not looking at Miss Mason or any of the girls. She knew that quite a lot of them were looking at *her*, though, wondering why she was back, and what had happened to her during the last few days.

And the answer to that last question was, quite a lot! She somehow had to try and forget it, though, or the memories of Leo Copeland were going to drive her more than a little crazy.

To her relief, the girls were sent up to their rooms quite early in the evening by Miss Mason, to pack their belongings ready for their departure in the morning. Ellie escaped to her own room, relieved to be on her own for a while. She just couldn't seem to cope with people right now, although she knew she was going to have to make an effort fairly soon.

She didn't need to pack since she hadn't even bothered to unpack in the first place. In fact, there was nothing for her to do except shower and go to bed. Wearily she made her way into the bathroom, stood under the hot water for a long time, then slowly dried herself. She pulled on a thin cotton nightie, brushed a little of the gloss back into her hair, then left the bathroom.

As she walked back into the bedroom, though, she was stunned to hear the sound of Leo's voice.

'I thought you were going to be in there all night,' he said calmly.

For a moment she thought she was hallucinating. Then her eyes met a tawny gaze that was hauntingly familiar, and her nerve-ends quivered in recognition.

He was standing by the window, not moving, not smiling; in fact, not doing *anything* except looking at her. Ellie's legs felt as if they were going to give way completely. Then, with a tremendous effort, she somehow recovered herself.

'What are you doing here?' she demanded. 'How did you find me?'

'I was sure you'd come back to Cairo and I took a chance that you'd booked into the same hotel. And I was right.' His gaze met and held hers. 'It's almost as if you wanted me to find you, Ellie.'

'I did not! And I want you to get out of here!' she snapped. 'I've just managed to get my old job back. If Miss Mason walks in and finds you here, I'm going to lose it again.'

Leo looked unconcerned. 'I think there are more important things to consider right now than your job.'

'Well, I don't! Miss Mason's given me one more chance, and I don't intend to blow it, so just get out of here.'

Leo continued to look as immovable as a mountain, though. Ellie gave a small sigh of pure despair. This whole situation was getting completely nightmarish. Every time she made any kind of effort to get her life back on to some kind of even keel, Leo walked in and tipped it upside-down again. Well, she had had enough! This was the last time he was going to do it to her.

'If you won't leave, then *I'm* going to walk out,' she said with some determination.

'Last time we were in this hotel, you tried to walk out on me wearing just a bathrobe,' he reminded her gently. 'This time you're only wearing a nightdress. I do seem to have an odd sort of effect on you, Ellie.'

Ellie stared down at herself. She had completely forgotten that she had been about to go to bed.

'It'll take me only a few seconds to get dressed,' she muttered. '*Then* I'll get out of here.'

'Why not stay and listen to what I've got to say?' Leo invited.

But she didn't think that was at all a good idea. Leo had a silver tongue—she had already learnt that, to her cost! And, on top of that, he was obviously a pretty accomplished liar. Look at the way she had swallowed his story about being a professional photographer, and believed she would be receiving a genuine salary. The truth was a lot more sordid, though. In reality, Leo had simply been paying for something that he had seen and wanted—and finally got!

'If you like, I'll apologise for everything that's happened so far,' he offered, remaining exactly where he was, as if he didn't want to frighten her by making any kind of move towards her.

'And you think that'll make everything all right?' Ellie demanded incredulously.

'I think it would at least be a start. I also think you're blowing this whole thing up out of proportion. All right, I told you a few lies. If it's any consolation to you, I felt badly about it at the time, and I had every intention of coming clean as soon as the right opportunity came up.'

'And when exactly was that right opportunity going to be?' she demanded with heavy sarcasm.

'I had the feeling you weren't going to take it too well, so I was waiting for a good moment.'

She shot a scornful glance at him. 'I'm sure you were! Didn't it ever occur to you that it would have been a lot simpler if you hadn't told the lies in the first place?'

'Yes, it did,' Leo agreed drily. 'But you were the one who assumed I was a professional photographer. I just decided to go along with it for a while, because it seemed a good way of holding your interest.'

Ellie stared at him in amazement. 'So now you're saying that it was all *my* fault? Because I jumped to the wrong conclusion, *I'm* to blame for everything that followed?'

A little of the calmness began to leave his face, and a warning light shone at the back of his eyes.

'Don't keep twisting things, Ellie. I never said you were to blame. I know I was the one who behaved badly. I'm just saying I only did it because there was something about you that made me want to get to know you a lot better.'

'Well, you certainly managed to do that!' she threw at him with dark meaning. 'Of course, it cost you quite a lot, but you look like a man who's willing to pay for what he wants!'

And this time Leo's gaze burned brightly.

'I've never paid a woman to go to bed with me, and I certainly had no intention of paying you!' he growled. 'If you'd just use your head instead of being so damned emotional about this, you'd realise that.'

'Oh, so sorry for being emotional,' she retorted. 'I suppose you'd like me to try and be as cool about the whole thing as you are.'

'I'm not cool, Ellie,' he said tightly. 'Don't make the mistake of thinking I am.'

For the first time, she looked straight at him instead of letting her gaze just flicker edgily over him. She saw the taut line of his mouth, the hard set of his muscles and the small nerve that ticked in his temple.

She swallowed hard. She suddenly realised that he was dangerously strung-up, that his earlier calmness had been nothing more than a façade.

'You want an explanation for the way I behaved?' he went on in a brittle voice. 'Well, I don't know if I've got one that will satisfy you, but I'm willing to have a go.' He shifted position, but then stood still again as he saw her flinch nervously. 'When I first saw you in the Egyptian Museum, my first thought was that you'd be perfect for the photo assignment I'd agreed to undertake. And, despite what you seem to think, it *was* a genuine assignment. I've a friend who runs a travel agency. When he heard I was coming to Egypt for a holiday, he asked me if I'd take some photos for the new set of brochures he's producing. Since photography is my main interest, I agreed at once. Taking pictures as I travelled around would be no problem. In fact, it would make the trip more interesting, as far as I was concerned.

'So you were going to take some snapshots while you were on holiday——' Ellie muttered.

'Not just "snapshots",' Leo cut in shortly. 'I regarded it as a job of work, and my friend insisted on paying me the standard rate for this sort of assignment. Not that I needed the money. I intended to give it to charity once I was back home.'

'How generous of you! But according to your friend Philip, you can well afford to be charitable. I believe you own a highly successful computer software company.'

'Damn Philip and his gossiping tongue,' Leo said darkly. 'After you'd gone, I reasoned that you had to have been talking to him. What did you do? Meet up with him that afternoon in Luxor, when you went out shopping?' His gaze burned even more fiercely. 'If you wanted the facts, why didn't you come to *me*?'

'Because you're not too hot on facts,' Ellie reminded him angrily. 'I never really seemed to know anything about you. And now that I do, I don't much like what I've found out!'

'Perhaps that's because you haven't let me finish my explanation of what happened.'

'What's there to explain? You saw me, decided to pick me up and have some fun with me. You must have had a good laugh when I fell for all those lines you spun me!'

'I've never laughed at you, Ellie,' said Leo, his voice suddenly becoming quiet. 'And, although I was originally interested in you because I knew you'd be a perfect photographic model, it soon became a lot more than that. The more time I spent with you, the more I discovered I liked being with you. And at the same time you intrigued me. There was something about you that hooked me. I knew I didn't want to let you just walk out of my life.'

'So you arranged for me to lose my job. Then you dangled a proposition in front of me that you knew I wouldn't be able to refuse,' she said bitterly. 'Couldn't *afford* to refuse, after I was fired.'

'I didn't deliberately set out to get you the sack. But when it happened, I realised it could be one of the best things that had ever happened to you. You struck me as a girl who needed to be cut free, to have some fun. And you certainly weren't going to have any fun while Miss Mason was around,' he finished wryly.

'You are unbelievably arrogant!' Ellie accused. 'You always think *you* know what's best for me.'

'But I was right, wasn't I, Ellie?' he said in a soft tone. 'You did hate that job. And we did have fun together. More than that, though, I think I might be able to give you a few things that you need. You've had a lousy time of it during much of your life, and now you've ended up completely on your own. That isn't a good situation for a girl like you to be in. You need someone to talk to, and laugh with. Someone who'll be a friend as well as a lover.'

'And you're volunteering for that job?'

'It rather looks like it,' Leo said levelly.

'Thanks, but I don't need anyone to feel sorry for me,' Ellie threw back at him.

'I didn't say I felt sorry for you.'

For just a moment, she almost allowed herself to hope. Then her eyes grew dull again.

'Whatever you think you feel, it wouldn't work. You're a liar, Leo, and I hate people who deliberately lie to me. And I hate you for what you've done to me.'

'And what *have* I done to you, Ellie?' he asked her quietly.

You've made me need you. You've made me *love* you, she wanted to scream at him with sudden vehemence. Instead, she answered him in a flat tone.

'You've turned my life into an even worse mess than it was in before. And I really didn't think that was possible.'

He gave an oddly helpless shrug of his shoulders. 'I don't know what else to say to you. I've apologised to you. And I've told you the truth.'

'I know,' she said, refusing to look at him.

'What more do you want from me?'

Ellie closed her eyes. Quite suddenly she had had enough of this. She couldn't take it for one more second.

'I want you to leave me alone,' she said in a low whisper.

And when she opened her eyes again, she found Leo had gone.

Ellie didn't sleep at all that night, and moved around the next morning in a numb daze. Why had she sent Leo away like that? She didn't know. She suspected it was because she was too much of a coward to do anything else. Everything had happened too fast, become too confused, ended in too much turmoil. She couldn't cope with it—couldn't cope with Leo.

As the school party got ready to leave the hotel, she spoke to people, answered queries from the girls and obeyed instructions from Miss Mason, but without taking any of it in. She supposed she wasn't talking complete gibberish or someone would have noticed by now, but she couldn't remember a single word she had said to anyone. She seemed to be operating on some sort of automatic pilot, and she just hoped it would keep going for a while longer. It would be really embarrassing and humiliating if she collapsed into a gibbering heap in front of everyone.

A minibus took them to the airport, which was hot and crowded. Their luggage went off in one direction, while Ellie, Miss Mason and the group of girls checked in and then waited for their flight to be called.

When the announcement finally came, Ellie got tiredly to her feet and trailed after the rest of the party as they headed towards the departure gate. She was going home. And, right now, it felt like the very last place on earth she wanted to go.

As they neared the gate, she raised her gaze and looked ahead for the first time. And that was when she saw the familiar figure standing in front of the barrier.

She couldn't quite believe it. Then she began to feel the first tremors of trepidation. She didn't want another confrontation with Leo. Not here; not in front of everyone. Scenes were bad enough when they were conducted in private. Anyway, just Leo's presence could well cost her her job, because she could already see Miss Mason's back stiffening as she recognised the man lying in wait for Ellie.

Leo stepped forward, totally ignoring Miss Mason's hostile glare.

'I think we've some unfinished business, Ellie,' he stated firmly.

'We do not! Please go away,' she said, almost pleadingly. 'I've nothing more to say to you.'

'Well, there's quite a lot I want to say to you,' he stated firmly. 'I would have said it last night, but you were obviously too exhausted to take any more——'

'Last night?' cut in Miss Mason sharply. 'Miss Mitchell, am I to understand that you were with this man last night?'

'Please don't interrupt,' Leo told her, politely but very firmly. 'This is absolutely none of your business.'

Loud gasps came from the group of girls. *No one* spoke to Miss Mason like that!

'Ellie, I'm going to say just a couple of things to you, and then you're going to have to make a decision,' Leo went on. 'First, I want you to know that I will never lie to you again. Second, I want to tell you that the night we spent together was the most special of my life. And third—and perhaps the most important—I love you and want you to stay with me.'

Ellie just stared at him. 'You—you love me?' she finally managed to croak.

'Of course. And I've got an entire family who are going to love you, just as soon as they get to know you.'

She opened her mouth to say something else, but absolutely nothing came out.

Miss Mason could certainly find something to say, though.

'Miss Mitchell, I will not have you discussing your personal affairs in front of these girls!'

Leo turned to her. 'I've already asked you to stay out of this,' he reminded her. 'Let Ellie decide if she wants to go back to a dull job and an even duller future, or if she wants to come with me.' His tawny gaze swung back to rest on Ellie. 'Time to make your choice,' he told her softly. 'Are you going to play it safe, Ellie? Or are you going to risk everything, and try marriage to me?'

'M-marriage?' she stuttered, her eyes flying wide open.

He suddenly grinned. 'It's the only proposal I dare make in front of Miss Mason!' Then his face became more serious. 'I didn't mean to say anything like that to you for some time yet. And I know there are still a hundred and one things that we need to talk about and sort out. I don't want to risk losing you, though, so I want you to know exactly where I stand—and what I'm offering you. Of course, you might not be ready for that sort of commitment yet. I'll give you more time, if you want it.'

Ellie was still blinking dazedly. The shock was slowly beginning to wear off now, though, and she knew she would never get another offer like this in her entire life. If she didn't find the courage to accept it, she would forever regret it.

'No,' she whispered. 'No—I don't think I want more time.'

His eyes became intense. 'Then which is it to be, Ellie. Yes or no?'

'Yes,' she said in a low voice, not quite believing that she was actually agreeing to marry Leo Copeland.

And in front of a *very* interested audience, in the middle of a busy airport!

'You'll regret that decision,' Miss Mason warned her.

'No, she won't,' Leo replied at once. 'I'll make sure of that. And now, if you don't want your group of girls to be totally shocked, you'd better take them away pretty quickly, because I intend to very thoroughly kiss my future wife.'

He moved forward and firmly scooped Ellie into his arms. And as he did so the entire group of girls burst into loud cheers and applause.

Miss Mason vainly tried to keep order, and finally managed to steer them through the departure gate and towards their waiting plane. Ellie didn't see them go, though, because by then Leo was already carrying out his threat to kiss her.

She couldn't resist the touch of his lips, any more than she had been able to resist his proposal. It was crazy, of course. In fact, the whole thing was crazy. Yet it felt so completely right, and perhaps that was the only important thing in the end.

Leo's hands held her up as she sagged a little weakly against him.

'Is all this for real?' she asked him rather wonderingly.

'It certainly is,' he assured her. 'I'll admit it's all been rather rushed and unorthodox, but I think I knew what I wanted from the first moment I saw you. And now it looks as if you want the same thing. Although I didn't think I was ever going to get you to admit it!' he added drily.

'Perhaps you should have tried kissing me,' Ellie murmured. 'That way, you can get me to admit to just about anything.'

'I did think of it,' admitted Leo. 'But I've got a certain amount of male pride. I wanted you to want *me*, not just a good time in bed.'

Ellie's eyes suddenly sparkled. 'Can't I have both?'

'You most certainly can,' he confirmed huskily. His mouth returned to hers, searching restlessly for a response and instantly finding it. His hands slid from her waist to just below the curve of her breast, then he gave a frustrated groan as he remembered where they were.

'This is no way to behave in the middle of an airport. It's just making me want something I can't have. At least, not right now,' he added, with a suddenly wicked grin. 'But as soon as I get you somewhere where we can be completely on our own——'

Ellie's heart did a funny double flip, and she wondered if it was ever going to beat at its normal rate again. It certainly went haywire whenever Leo was around, and he seemed determined to stick very close in the future.

She stared up into his tawny eyes, and was surprised to find he looked almost as dazed as she did.

'I think the shock's just beginning to hit me,' he murmured, a wry smile twisting him mouth. 'Meeting someone and proposing all in little more than a week—I definitely didn't have anything like that planned when I first set out for Egypt!'

'Nor did I,' said Ellie with an answering grin. Then she looked a little anxious. 'You're sure you don't want to change your mind? I mean, this is all pretty sudden——'

'I'm absolutely certain,' he said firmly. 'And as for the shock—we've got the rest of our lives to get over that.'

The rest of their lives—Ellie liked the sound of that. And, when Leo held out his hand to her, she slid her fingers into his without hesitation, and let him lead her off to a future that suddenly seemed incredibly bright.

Take 4 bestselling love stories FREE
Plus get a FREE surprise gift!

Special Limited-time Offer

Mail to
Harlequin Reader Service®
3010 Walden Avenue
P.O. Box 1867
Buffalo, N.Y. 14269-1867

YES! Please send me 4 free Harlequin Presents® novels and my free surprise gift. Then send me 6 brand-new novels every month, which I will receive months before they appear in bookstores. Bill me at the low price of $2.47 each—a savings of 28¢ apiece off cover prices. There are no shipping, handling or other hidden costs. I understand that accepting the books and gift places me under no obligation ever to buy any books. I can always return a shipment and cancel at any time. Even if I never buy another book from Harlequin, the 4 free books and the surprise gift are mine to keep forever.

106 BPA AC9K

Name	(PLEASE PRINT)	
Address		Apt. No.
City	State	Zip

This offer is limited to one order per household and not valid to present Harlequin Presents® subscribers. Terms and prices are subject to change. Sales tax applicable in N.Y.

PRES-BPA2DR   © 1990 Harlequin Enterprises Limited

HARLEQUIN®
OFFICIAL SWEEPSTAKES
RULES

NO PURCHASE NECESSARY

1. To enter, complete an Official Entry Form or 3"× 5" index card by hand-printing, in plain block letters, your complete name, address, phone number and age, and mailing it to: Harlequin Fashion A Whole New You Sweepstakes, P.O. Box 9056, Buffalo, NY 14269-9056.

   No responsibility is assumed for lost, late or misdirected mail. Entries must be sent separately with first class postage affixed, and be received no later than December 31, 1991 for eligibility.

2. Winners will be selected by D.L. Blair, Inc., an independent judging organization whose decisions are final, in random drawings to be held on January 30, 1992 in Blair, NE at 10:00 a.m. from among all eligible entries received.

3. The prizes to be awarded and their approximate retail values are as follows: Grand Prize — A brand-new Mercury Sable LS plus a trip for two (2) to Paris, including round-trip air transportation, six (6) nights hotel accommodation, a $1,400 meal/spending money stipend and $2,000 cash toward a new fashion wardrobe (approximate value: $28,000) or $15,000 cash; two (2) Second Prizes — A trip to Paris, including round-trip air transportation, six (6) nights hotel accommodation, a $1,400 meal/spending money stipend and $2,000 cash toward a new fashion wardrobe (approximate value: $11,000) or $5,000 cash; three (3) Third Prizes — $2,000 cash toward a new fashion wardrobe. All prizes are valued in U.S. currency. Travel award air transportation is from the commercial airport nearest winner's home. Travel is subject to space and accommodation availability, and must be completed by June 30, 1993. Sweepstakes offer is open to residents of the U.S. and Canada who are 21 years of age or older as of December 31, 1991, except residents of Puerto Rico, employees and immediate family members of Torstar Corp., its affiliates, subsidiaries, and all agencies, entities and persons connected with the use, marketing, or conduct of this sweepstakes. All federal, state, provincial, municipal and local laws apply. Offer void wherever prohibited by law. Taxes and/or duties, applicable registration and licensing fees, are the sole responsibility of the winners. Any litigation within the province of Quebec respecting the conduct and awarding of a prize may be submitted to the Régie des loteries et courses du Québec. All prizes will be awarded; winners will be notified by mail. No substitution of prizes is permitted.

4. Potential winners must sign and return any required Affidavit of Eligibility/Release of Liability within 30 days of notification. In the event of noncompliance within this time period, the prize may be awarded to an alternate winner. Any prize or prize notification returned as undeliverable may result in the awarding of that prize to an alternate winner. By acceptance of their prize, winners consent to use of their names, photographs or their likenesses for purposes of advertising, trade and promotion on behalf of Torstar Corp. without further compensation. Canadian winners must correctly answer a time-limited arithmetical question in order to be awarded a prize.

5. For a list of winners (available after 3/31/92), send a separate stamped, self-addressed envelope to: Harlequin Fashion A Whole New You Sweepstakes, P.O. Box 4694, Blair, NE 68009.

PREMIUM OFFER TERMS

To receive your gift, complete the Offer Certificate according to directions. Be certain to enclose the required number of "Fashion A Whole New You" proofs of product purchase (which are found on the last page of every specially marked "Fashion A Whole New You" Harlequin or Silhouette romance novel). Requests must be received no later than December 31, 1991. Limit: four (4) gifts per name, family, group, organization or address. Items depicted are for illustrative purposes only and may not be exactly as shown. Please allow 6 to 8 weeks for receipt of order. Offer good while quantities of gifts last. In the event an ordered gift is no longer available, you will receive a free, previously unpublished Harlequin or Silhouette book for every proof of purchase you have submitted with your request, plus a refund of the postage and handling charge you have included. Offer good in the U.S. and Canada only.

HOFW · SWPR

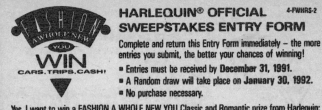

HARLEQUIN® OFFICIAL SWEEPSTAKES ENTRY FORM

4-FWHRS-2

Complete and return this Entry Form immediately – the more entries you submit, the better your chances of winning!

- Entries must be received by **December 31, 1991.**
- A Random draw will take place on **January 30, 1992.**
- No purchase necessary.

Yes, I want to win a FASHION A WHOLE NEW YOU Classic and Romantic prize from Harlequin:

Name _____ Telephone _____ Age _____

Address _____

City _____ State _____ Zip _____

Return Entries to: **Harlequin FASHION A WHOLE NEW YOU,**
P.O. Box 9056, Buffalo, NY 14269-9056   © 1991 Harlequin Enterprises Limited

PREMIUM OFFER

To receive your free gift, send us the required number of proofs-of-purchase from any specially marked FASHION A WHOLE NEW YOU Harlequin or Silhouette Book with the Offer Certificate properly completed, plus a check or money order (do not send cash) to cover postage and handling payable to Harlequin FASHION A WHOLE NEW YOU Offer. We will send you the specified gift.

OFFER CERTIFICATE

Item	A. ROMANTIC COLLECTOR'S DOLL (Suggested Retail Price $60.00)	B. CLASSIC PICTURE FRAME (Suggested Retail Price $25.00)
# of proofs-of-purchase	18	12
Postage and Handling	$3.50	$2.95
Check one	☐	☐

Name _____

Address _____

City _____ State _____ Zip _____

Mail this certificate, designated number of proofs-of-purchase and check or money order for postage and handling to: **Harlequin FASHION A WHOLE NEW YOU Gift Offer,** P.O. Box 9057, Buffalo, NY 14269-9057. Requests must be received by December 31, 1991.

ONE PROOF-OF-PURCHASE
4-FWHRP-2

To collect your fabulous free gift you must include the necessary number of proofs-of-purchase with a properly completed Offer Certificate.

© 1991 Harlequin Enterprises Limited

See previous page for details.

Fall in love with

 ### *Harlequin Superromance*®

Passionate.
Love that strikes like lightning. Drama that will touch your heart.

Provocative.
As new and exciting as today's headlines.

Poignant.
Stories of men and women like you. People who affirm the values of loving, caring and commitment in today's complex world.

At 300 pages, Superromance novels will give you even more hours of enjoyment.

Look for four new titles every month.

Harlequin Superromance
"Books that will make you laugh and cry."

SUPER